The WOMAN WHO WAITED

Also by Andreï Makine

A Hero's Daughter
Confessions of a Fallen Standard-Bearer
Once Upon the River Love
Dreams of My Russian Summers
The Crime of Olga Arbyelina
Requiem for a Lost Empire
Music of a Life
The Earth and Sky of Jacques Dorme

The WOMAN WHO WAITED

A Novel

Andreï Makine

Translated from the French by Geoffrey Strachan

ARCADE PUBLISHING
NEW YORK

FIRST ENGLISH-LANGUAGE EDITION

First published in France as *La Femme qui attendait* by Editions du Seuil

This is a work of fiction. Names, characters, places, and incidents are either the work of the author's imagination or are used fictitiously.

Library of Congress Cataloging-in-Publication Data

Makine, Andreï, 1957–
[Femme qui attendait. English]
The woman who waited : a novel / by Andreï Makine ; translated from the French by Geoffrey Strachan. —1st English-language ed.
p. cm.
ISBN 1-55970-774-7
I. Strachan, Geoffrey. II. Title.

PQ2673.A38416F4613 2006
843'.914—dc22 2005010314

Published in the United States by Arcade Publishing, Inc., New York
Distributed by Time Warner Book Group

Visit our Web site at www.arcadepub.com

10 9 8 7 6 5 4 3 2 1

Designed by API

EB

PRINTED IN THE UNITED STATES OF AMERICA

TRANSLATOR'S NOTE

ANDREÏ MAKINE WAS BORN AND BROUGHT UP in Russia, but *The Woman Who Waited*, like his other novels, was written in French. The book is set in Russia, and the author uses some Russian words in the French text, which I have kept in this English translation. These include *nyet* (no), *izba* (a traditional wooden house built of logs), *dacha* (a country house or cottage, typically used as a second or holiday home), and *sarafan* (a traditional sleeveless tunic dress).

There are also a number of references to well-known Russian place names, including the Nevsky Prospekt, the street in St. Petersburg (Leningrad under the Soviet Union), and to institutions from the Communist era in Russia. A kolkhoz was a collective farm, a kolkhoznik a member of the farm collective. An apparatchik was a member of the party administration, or *apparat*. References from French cultural life include those to Jean-Luc Godard, the influential New Wave film director of the 1960s, the events of May 1968, when student protests in France led to a crisis that shook the government, and Colonel Chabert, the eponymous hero of Balzac's 1834 novel, who returns from the war in which he was reported killed to find his wife has remarried and refuses to recognize him.

G.S.

One

"SHE IS A WOMAN so intensely destined for happiness (if only purely physical happiness, mere bodily well-being), and yet she has chosen, almost casually, it seems, solitude, loyalty to an absent one, a refusal to love. . . ."

This is the sentence I wrote down at that crucial moment when we believe we have sized up another person (this woman, Vera). Up to that point, all is curiosity, guesswork, a hankering after confessions. Hunger for the other person, the lure of her hidden depths. But once their secret has been decoded, along come these words, often pretentious and dogmatic, dissecting, pinpointing, categorizing. It all becomes comprehensible, reassuring. Now the routine of a relationship, or of indifference, can take over. The other one's mystery has been tamed. Her body reduced to a flesh-and-blood mechanism, desirable or not. Her heart to a set of predictable responses.

At this stage, in fact, a kind of murder occurs, for we kill this being of infinite and inexhaustible potential we have encountered. We would rather deal with a verbal construct than a living person. . . .

It must have been during those September days, in a village among forests stretching all the way to the White Sea, that I noted down observations of this type: "a being of inexhaustible potential," "murder," "a woman stripped naked by words." At the time (I was twenty-six), such conclusions struck me as wonderfully perceptive. I took great pride in having gained insight into the secret life of a woman old enough to be my mother, in having summed up her destiny in a few well-turned phrases. I thought about her smile, the wave she greeted me with when she caught sight of me in the distance on the shore of the lake, the love she could have given so many men but gave no one. "A woman so intensely destined for happiness . . ." Yes, I was pretty pleased with my analysis. I even recalled a nineteenth-century critic referring to a "dialectic of the soul" to describe the art with which writers probe the contradictions of the human psyche: "A woman destined for happiness, but . . ."

That September evening I closed my notebook,

glanced at the handful of cold, mottled cranberries Vera had deposited on my table in my absence. Outside the window, above the dark treetops of the forest, the sky still had a milky pallor suggestive of the somnolent presence, a few hours' walk away, of the White Sea, where winter already loomed. Vera's house was located at the start of a path that led to the coast by way of thickets and hills. Reflecting on this woman's isolation, her tranquillity, her body (very physically, I imagined a tapered sheath of soft warmth surrounding that female body beneath the covers on a clear night of hoarfrost), I suddenly grasped that no "dialectic of the soul" was capable of telling the secret of this life. A life all too plain and woefully simple compared to these intellectual analyses of mine.

The life of a woman waiting for the one she loved. No other mystery.

The only puzzling but rather trivial element was the mistake I made: following our first encounter at the end of August, which lasted only a few seconds, I had encountered Vera again at the beginning of September. And I had failed to recognize her. I was convinced these were two different women.

Yet both of them struck me as "so intensely destined for happiness . . ."

Later, I would get to know the ups and downs of the pathways, the trees' vivid attire, new at every twist in the road, the fleeting curves of the lake, whose shoreline I was soon able to follow with my eyes closed. But on that end-of-summer day, I was only beginning to know the area, taking random walks, happily if uneasily, aware that I might end up discovering an abandoned village within this larch forest, or crossing some half-rotten wooden footbridge like a tightrope walker. In fact, it was at the entrance to an apparently uninhabited village that I saw her.

At first I thought I had surprised a couple making love. Amid the undergrowth covering the shores of the lake, I glimpsed the intense white gleam of a thigh, the curve of a torso straining with effort, I heard breathless panting. The evening was still light, but the sun was low and its raw red streaked the scene with shadow and fire, setting the willow leaves ablaze. At the heart of all this turmoil, a woman's face was suddenly visible, almost grazing the clay soil with her chin, then all at once catapulted backward, amid a wild surge of hair tossed aside. . . . The air was hot, sticky. The last heat of the season, an Indian summer, borne there these past few days by the south wind.

I was about to continue on my way when suddenly the branches shook and the woman appeared, inclined her head in a vague greeting, and rapidly straightened up her dress, which had ridden up above her knees. I greeted her awkwardly in turn, unable to form a clear view of her face, on which the glow from the setting sun alternated with stripes of shadow. At her feet, forming a heap like the body of a drowned man, lay the coils of a large fishing net she had just hauled in.

For several seconds we remained rooted to the spot, bound by an ambiguous complicity, like that of a hurried sexual encounter in a risky location or a criminal act. I stared at her bare feet, reddened by the clay, and at the twitching bulk of the net: the greenish bodies of several pike were thrashing about heavily, and at the top, tangled among the floaters, extended the long, almost black curve of what I at first took to be a snake (probably an eel or a young catfish). This mass of cords and fish was slowly draining, water mingled with russet slime flowing toward the lake like a fine trickle of blood. The atmosphere was heavy, as before a storm. The still air imprisoned us in fixed postures, the paralysis of a nightmare. And there was a shared perception, tacit and instinctive, that between this man and this woman, at this red and violent nightfall, anything could happen. Absolutely anything. And there was nothing and no one to prevent it. Their bodies could lie down beside the tangle of the net, melt into one another, take their pleasure, even as the lives trapped in the fishnet breathed their last. . . .

I retreated swiftly, with a feeling that, out of cowardice, I had sidestepped the moment when destiny manifests itself at a particular spot, in a particular face. The moment when fate allows us a glimpse of its hidden tissue of cause and consequence.

A week later, retribution: a northeast wind brought the first snow, as if in revenge for those few days of paradise. A mild retribution, however, in the form of luminous white flurries that induced vertigo, blurring the views of road and field, making people smile, dazzled by endlessly swirling snowflakes. The bitter, tangy air tasted of new hope, the promise of happiness. The squalls hurled volleys of crystals onto the dark surface of the lake, which relentlessly swallowed their fragile whiteness into its depths. But already the shorelines were gleaming with snow, and the muddy scars left on the road by our truck were swiftly bandaged over.

The driver with whom I often traveled from one village to the next used to declare himself, ironically, to be "the first swallow of capitalism." Otar, a Georgian of about forty, had set up a clandestine fur business, been denounced, done time in prison. Now out on parole, he had been given charge of this old truck with worm-eaten side panels here in this northern territory. We were in the mid-seventies, and this "first swallow of capitalism" sincerely believed he had come out of things pretty well. "And what's more," he would often repeat, with shining eyes and a greedy smile, "for every guy up here there are nine chicks."

He talked about women incessantly, lived for women, and I conjectured that even his fur business had had as its object the chance to dress and undress women. Intelligent in fact, and even sensitive, he naturally exaggerated his vocation as a philanderer, knowing that such was the image of Georgians in Russia: lovers obsessed with conquests, monomaniacal about sex, rich, unsophisticated. He acted out this caricature, as foreigners often do when they end up mimicking the tourist clichés of their country of origin. He played to the gallery.

Despite this roleplaying, for him the female body was, naturally, logically, the only thing that made life worthwhile. And it would have been the worst form of torture not to be able to talk about it to a well-disposed confidant. Willy-nilly I had assumed this role. In gratitude, Otar was ready to take me to the North Pole.

In his stories, he somehow or other contrived to avoid repetition. And yet they invariably dealt with women, desired, seduced, possessed. He took them lying down, standing up, hunched up in the cab of his truck, spread-eagled against a cowshed wall as the drowsy beasts chewed their cuds, in a forest glade at the base of an anthill ("We both had our backsides bitten to death by those buggers!"), in steam baths. . . . His language was both coarse and ornate: he made "that great ass split open like a watermelon," and in the baths "breasts swell up, you know, they really do, like dough rising"; "I shoved her up against a cherry tree. I penetrated her, shook her so hard a whole shitload of cherries showered down on top of us. We were all red with juice. . . ." At heart he was a veritable poet of the flesh, and the sincerity of his passion for the female body rescued his stories from coital monotony.

One day, I was foolish enough to ask him how I could tell whether a woman was ready to accept my advances or not. "If she fucks?" he exclaimed, giving a twist to the steering wheel. "No problem. Just ask her one simple question. . . ." Like a good actor, he let the pause linger, visibly content to be instructing a young simpleton. "All you need to know is this. Does she eat smoked herring?"

"Smoked herring? Why?"

"Here's why: if she eats smoked herring, she gets thirsty. . . ."

"So?"

"And if she's thirsty, she drinks a lot of water."

"I don't follow."

"Well, if she drinks water, she pisses. Right?"

"Yes. And so?"

"So if she pisses, she must have a twat."

"Well, all right, but . . ."

"And if she has a twat, she fucks!"

He went into a long laugh that drowned out the noise of the engine, thumped me several times on the shoulder, oblivious of the flurry of flakes sweeping across the road. This all happened on that same day of that first snow in early September. We had just arrived at an apparently deserted village, which I failed to recognize—neither the *izbas* transfigured by their snowy coating nor the shores of the lake all carpeted in white.

Otar braked, seized a bucket, went over to a well. His antediluvian truck bizarrely consumed as much water as gas. "Like that chick who eats smoked herring," he joked, winking at me knowingly.

We were about to continue on our way when they appeared. Two female figures, one tall and quite youthful, the other a tiny old woman, were climbing up the slope that led from the lake to the road. They had just been taking a bath in the minuscule *izba* from whose chimney a haze of smoke still filtered. The old woman walked with difficulty, struggling against the gusts of wind, turning her face aside from the volleys of snow. Her companion looked almost as if she were carrying her. She was dressed in a long military greatcoat of the type once worn in the cavalry. She was bareheaded (perhaps, surprised by the snow, she had given her shawl to the old woman), and against the heavy fabric of the coat collar, her neck looked almost childishly slender. Reaching the road, they turned toward the village; we could see them full face now. At that moment, a gust of wind more violent than the rest blew back one of the sides of the long cavalry greatcoat, and for the space of a second we saw the whiteness of a breast, swiftly covered up by the woman as she tugged irritably at her coat lapels.

Without starting the engine, Otar stared fixedly through the open door. I was waiting for his observation. I remembered his "breasts swell up, you know, at the baths . . ." I was sure I was going to have to listen to a hilarious, racy monologue along those lines. And for the first time I foresaw that such talk, albeit jocular and good-natured, would be painful to me.

But he did not stir, his hands on the wheel, his eyes fixed on the two female shapes as they were gradually blotted out by the snow flurry. . . .

His voice rang out just as he eased the clutch and the mud spurted from beneath the spinning wheels. "That blessed Vera! She's still waiting! Still waiting! She'll wait forever. . . . She's screwed up her whole life with her waiting! He was killed or was reported missing in action, same difference. You cry your heart out, okay. You down a few vodkas, okay. You wear black, fine, it's the custom. But after that you start to live again. Life goes on, goddamn it! She was sixteen when he went to the front in 'forty-five, and she's been waiting ever since. Because they never got a reliable bit of paper about the guy's death. She's dug herself a grave here. Along with all these old women that no one gives a damn about, but she goes around picking up half-dead people in the middle of the forest. And she goes on waiting. . . . It's thirty years now, for fuck's sake! And you've seen what a beauty she is, even now. . . ."

He fell silent, then gave me a fierce look and cried out in a scathing voice: "Well, this isn't one of your smoked-herring stories, you stupid prick!" I almost responded in the same vein, thinking the oath was addressed to me, but held my peace. His despairing way of hitting the wheel with the flat of his hands showed it was himself he was angry with. His face lost its ruddy glow and turned gray. I sensed that, violent as he was in his refusal to understand this woman, at the same time, since he was a true mountain dweller, her waiting inspired in him the almost holy respect that is due to a vow, a solemn oath. . . .

We didn't exchange another word all the way to town, the district capital, where I climbed down. On the central square, covered in muddy snow, a young married couple, surrounded by their nearest and dearest, were just leaving the front steps of an administrative building to take their places in the leading car of a beribboned motorcade. In the sky, above the flat roof, above a faded red flag, a live triangle of wild geese flew past.

"You know, maybe she's right, after all, that Vera," Otar said to me, as I shook his hand. "In any case, it's not for me, or you for that matter, to judge her."

I did not attempt to "judge" her. I simply saw her from a great distance several days after that encounter in the snow, walking along the shore.

The day was limpid and icy: after the last spasms of a summer that had swung wildly from midsummer heat to snow squalls, autumn reigned. The snow had melted, the ground was dry and hard, the willow leaves glittered, slivers of gold in the blue air. I felt accepted by these sun-drenched meadows, the shadowy mass of the forest, the windows of a few *izbas*, which seemed to be staring at me with melancholy benevolence.

On the far shore of the lake I recognized her: a dark upright amid the chilly, gilded blaze. I followed her with my eyes for a long time, struck by a simple notion that made all other thoughts about her destiny pointless: "There goes a woman," I said to myself, "about whom I know everything. Her whole life is there before me, concentrated in that distant figure walking beside the lake.

She's a woman who's been waiting for the man she loves for thirty years, that is, from time immemorial."

The next day I set out to walk to the White Sea coast. One of the old women who lived in the village pointed out the path to me, partly overgrown by the forest, assuring me that in her youth it used to take her half a day to reach it, and that for me, with my long legs . . . Very near to the shoreline, I lost my way. Hoping to skirt a hill, I landed in a dank peat bog, floundered about among creeks from which a strong marshy smell arose. The ocean was very close at hand; from time to time the sour surface of the stagnant water was ruffled by a sea breeze . . . But the sun was already beginning to set; I had to resign myself to going home.

My return was like the retreat following a rout. No longer a known path, wild changes of direction, the ridiculous fear of being really lost, and the spiderwebs I had to keep wiping from my face, along with the salt sweat.

At the moment when I was least hoping for it, the village and the lake suddenly materialized, as if from a dream. A tranquil dream, aglow with the sunset's pale transparency. I sat down on a thick slab of granite, which must once have marked the boundary of an estate. In a few seconds, weariness flooded in, even banishing my irritation at having failed to reach my goal. I felt drained, absent, as if all that was left of me was this slow stare, sliding weightlessly across the world.

At the place where the path leading to the village met the road to the district capital, I saw Vera. At this crossroads, there was a small sign fixed to a post bearing the name of the village, Mirnoe. A little below this a mailbox had been nailed to it, empty for most of the time but occasionally harboring a local newspaper. Vera went up to the post, lifted the mailbox's tin flap, thrust her hand inside. Even from a long way off, I sensed that the gesture was not automatic, that it had still not become automatic. . . .

I recalled our first, abrupt encounter at the end of August. The huge fishing net, the glance from an unknown woman, her body hot from the exertion. My conviction that between us anything might have happened. My sense of having missed an opportunity. I had recorded it all in my notebook. Now those notes seemed utterly incongruous. The woman looking for a letter in a rusty mailbox lived on another planet.

It was from this planet that she greeted me as she approached, smiled, made her way toward her house. I thought about this wait of hers, and for the first time her fate seemed neither strange nor unusual to me.

"In fact, all women wait like her," I formulated

clumsily, "throughout their lives. All women, in every country, in every age. They wait for a man to appear, there at the end of the road, in this clear light of sunset. A man with a firm, serious look, returning from somewhere beyond death, to a woman who never gave up hope in spite of everything. And the ones who don't wait are mere smoked-herring eaters."

The aggressiveness of this conclusion made me feel better, for I had come to that village partly because of one of those women who were incapable of waiting.

2

I HAD COME TO ESCAPE from people who found our times too slow. But what I was really fleeing was myself, since I differed very little from them. I came to this conclusion one night in March, in the studio we used to call the Wigwam. A face there, sketched on a thinly painted canvas, bore a curious resemblance to my own.

At a certain moment, the tempo of the recitation coincided with the rhythmic panting of two lovers. Everyone tried to keep a straight face. Especially the poet himself, for the content of his verses demanded it. In them, our country was compared to a terrifying planet, whose vast bulk prevented anyone from breaking free from its gravitational pull. The word *planét* was rhymed with *nyet,* several times over, hammered out in an incantation. At the height of the declamation, this reiterated rhyme began to be echoed by masculine grunts, and, in a higher register, the moans of a woman: the couple separated from us only by a few canvases stacked on easels. Including the barely colored-in portrait of a man who looked like me.

The situation was farcical. And yet that night, though one of celebration like so many others spent in that studio, was a sad one.

As always, of course, there was plenty of alcohol, plenty of music (a jazz singer on the verge of whispering secrets into the ears of all and sundry but who continued to postpone his revelations), plenty of bodies, most of them young, ready to make love without constraint, or rather to make love in order to defy all constraints.

Six or seven years late, May '68 had finally made it to Russia, had made it to this long loft converted into a semi-clandestine studio in a remote suburb of Leningrad.

"Planét—Nyet!" declaimed the author of the poem and was answered from behind the unfinished paintings by the clamor of an imminent orgasm. *Nyet* was what stifled the maturing of talent, freedom of expression, unfettered love, foreign travel, everything, in fact. This loft alone was airborne, challenging the laws of gravity.

It was a typical setting for such gatherings of more

or less dissident artists. From Kiev to Vladivostok, from Leningrad to Tiflis, everyone was saying, fearing, hoping for approximately the same thing. It all usually took place amid the glee generated by secrecy and subversion, especially when one is young. And what could not be said in a poem or with a paintbrush, we expressed through these erratic orgasms. "Planét Nyet," and the moans now starting up again behind the canvases, louder than ever.

But on this occasion there was something forced about the gaiety. Even the presence of an American journalist made no difference. Having him there was a great event for us all: he sat in the middle, ensconced in an armchair; given the throng that surrounded him, he might have been taken for the president of the United States. But the chemistry was all wrong.

It would have been easy to ascribe the melancholy I felt to jealousy.

Hardly more than a week earlier, the woman now moaning behind the canvases had been sleeping with me. I knew the sound of her voice in lovemaking, and I could recognize her part in the current duet. Without flinching. Without the right to be jealous. Sexual ownership was the height of petty bourgeois absurdity. One drank, smoked with screwed up eyes (as in Godard's films), approved the reading of a poem, and, when the woman finally emerged from among the canvases, one winked at her, offered her a drink.... I recalled how she sometimes used to raise her eyebrows in her sleep, as if asking herself: "What's it all for?" Then her face would become vulnerable, childlike.... Best not to remember!

That evening, if the truth be told, we all felt our hearts were not in it. Perhaps just because of the American journalist. Too big a fish for this shabby studio, a visitor too eagerly desired. He was there like the supreme incarnation of the Western world we dreamed of, he listened and watched, and we all felt as if we were being transported to the far side of the iron curtain. Thanks to him, the lines of verse recited already seemed as if they had been published in London or New York, an unfinished painting was on the verge of being hung in a Parisian art gallery. We were acting out a scenario of artistic dissidence for him. And even the moans of pleasure from behind the easels were addressed to him personally.

He had, in fact, quite simply upstaged us all. I had come intending to talk about my trip to Tallin. At that time, the Baltic states were looked upon as the antechamber to the West. Arkady Gorin, the little dark-haired man sitting on the ground on an old paintbox, would have talked about his imminent departure for Israel, after six years of being refused a visa. But there was this American, and the mere grinding of his jaw, as he pronounced names like Philadelphia, Boston, Greenwich Village, made our own stories seem pretty thin. . . .

Even the poem in which Brezhnev's Kremlin was portrayed as a zoo full of prehistoric animals did not go down as well as expected. Mediocre actors, we were putting on a performance of the Western world, and he, as the director (a veritable Stanislavsky!), was sizing us up, ready to deliver the famous and terrible verdict: "I don't believe you." And it would have been fair: we were not very convincing westerners that night.

Too impatient. The iron curtain looked as if it would last forever. Our country's dislocation from the rest of the world had the semblance of some inviolable natural law. In the face of this thousand-year empire, our own youth was but a second, a speck of dust. We could no longer bear to wait.

All the more because every element of the Western world was available to us: irreverent poems, innovative abstract painting, uninhibited sexual gratification, the banned Western authors we purchased on the black market, the European and other languages we spoke, the Western thought we did our utmost to get to know. Like alchemists in a hurry, we tossed all these ingredients into the melting pot during our nights of boozing and declamation. The quintessence of the Western world would materialize, the philosopher's stone that would transform "The Kremlin Zoo" into a world masterpiece, its author into a living classic, acclaimed from New York to Sydney, and transfer that canvas covered in orange squares to the walls of the Guggenheim. . . .

A very drunk young woman collapsed onto the shabby mattress beside me. With a broad, wet smile, she was trying to whisper something in my ear, but her speech had become slurred. Two men's names kept recurring in her babble. I guessed, rather than understood, that two men were making love in the next room, and she found this "a scream," because at the same time we could hear the moaning of the couple behind the paintings. I pretended to chuckle in response to her laughter, but suddenly her face froze, she lowered her eyelids, and very tiny, swift tears began coursing down her cheeks. The jazz singer's grating whisper continued to promise great revelations without which life could not go on.

The woman stopped crying, gave me a challenging look, and made her way over toward where the American was sitting. "He's a very big gallery owner," the latter was saying. A painter listening to him nodded his head incessantly. His glass shook violently in his hand. The drunken young woman clambered up onto one arm of the chair with the persistence of an insect.

An evening that never quite took off . . .

Curiously enough, this copy of the Western world we were acting out was in some respects more authentic than the original. Above all, more fraught with drama. For the liberties taken on those evenings did not always go unpunished. Many years later, I would learn that the author of "The Kremlin Zoo" paid for his poem with five years in a camp and that one of the homosexuals, sent to prison (for this vice was punishable by law), was battered to death by his cellmates. I would think about that unfortunate lover fifteen years later in the streets of the Marais district of Paris; the multitude of bronzed, muscular men on the café terraces, their contented air, for all the world like chubby, male inflatable dolls, showing off their biceps and their new-won normality. I recalled that the homosexual from Leningrad had been finished off by being impaled on a stovepipe, from anus to throat. . . .

All things considered, our masquerade of the Western world did have its own weight of truth.

My girlfriend emerged from behind the canvases, made her way across the room strewn with bodies, fragments of food and bottles, and seated herself on a crate filled with books. Despite a mixture of disgust and jealousy, I could not repress a burst of admiration. What a great performance, much better than the women in Godard's films! A sensual body, a mouth with blurred makeup, and an impeccably indifferent look that slid right over me. And already she was flirting, accepting a drink, reveling in that quite special attentiveness men give to women who are ... "in heat," I thought maliciously. "No jealousy. No jealousy. You're being ridiculous, you great Siberian bear," a placatory voice kept repeating inside my head. I saw she had taken off her stockings. Her pale, bare legs suddenly seemed surprisingly youthful and touching, with their fair skin all unprotected, and the beauty spots whose pattern I knew well. A feeling of deep pity overcame me, I had an urge to go and cover those legs with my coat. . . .

That was when we noticed the American journalist was fast asleep. He had dozed off a moment before, his head slightly cocked to one side, and we had continued talking to him, taking his sleep for a posture of profound contemplation. We were addressing him in anticipation either of his approval or his Stanislavskian: "I don't believe you!" If he had snored, we would have burst out laughing and teased him. But he was sleeping like a baby, his eyes quietly closed, breathing through lips formed into a little oval. There was an embarrassed pause. I got up, went to the kitchen. As I made my way behind the canvases, I saw the man (he was a painter) who had just been making love with my late girlfriend. He was busy wiping his genitals with a cloth that smelled of turpentine. . . . The American journalist finally woke up, and from the kitchen I could hear his: "So . . . ," followed by a massive yawn and relieved guffaws from the others. . . .

The kitchen (in reality a continuation of the same loft, containing a sink with chipped enamel) had only one window, or rather a narrow skylight, with foodstuffs wrapped in sheets of newspaper piled up against it. The glass, which had a diagonal break in it, let through a fine dusting of snow, the last cold weather of winter.

At that moment, I felt I was living through precisely what I had been wanting to write about for a long time: the piquant acidity of the snow, an old building in a city at night on the shores of the Baltic, this loft, the utter isolation of the young man that I was, the proximity of voices so familiar, so alien, the swift fading, in this cold, of what had been my love for a woman who was at this very moment inviting another's caresses, the utter meaninglessness and irremediable seriousness of this fusion of bodies, the ridiculous transience of our time spent in cities, in other people's lives, in the void.

Something prevented me expressing it as I would have liked. "The regime!" we used to say during our clandestine evenings. *Planét Nyet.* Listening to the others, I had ended up convincing myself of this. The Kremlin Zoo blunted the sculptor's chisel, drained canvases of color, shackled rhymes. Censorship, we said. Conformist thinking. Ideological dictatorship. And it was true.

Yet, standing in front of the skylight with its broken panes that night, I began to have doubts. For no censorship stood in the way of my telling about this fine dusting of snow, loneliness, three o'clock in the morning in the darkness of a sleeping city on the Baltic coast. *Planét Nyet* seemed to me a somewhat facile argument now. To complain about the regime and not write, or to write purely to complain about it—here, I sensed, was the vicious circle of dissident literature.

I could not conceive (none of the guests at the Wigwam could) that ten years later cracks would start appearing in *Planét Nyet*, that fifteen years later it would shatter, losing its allies, its vassals, its frontiers, and even its name. And that one would then be able to write whatever one wanted without fear of censorship. One could linger beneath the broken skylight in a loft, at night in a sleeping city, feel powdery snow on one's face flushed with wine, reflect on the fleeting nature of our passage through the lives of other people. . . .

But in this future, exactly as it was in the past, it would be just as difficult for a poet to speak of these simple things: love for a woman who has ceased to love, snow on a March night, the condensation from a breath as it vanishes in the cold air and makes us think: "That's my life," that tenuous haze of anxiety and hope.

In fifteen years' time, the regime would no longer exist, but stanzas would not have an easier birth because of it, nor would poems be read more. No American journalists now to listen to the lines of verse being declaimed by tipsy poets, no danger now for the bold. And even the moaning behind the unfinished canvases would lose its shrill, provocative savor.

During that night of the last great frosts, I believed I had understood the aggravating paradox of art under a totalitarian regime: "Dictatorship is often conducive to the tragic creation of masterpieces. . . ."

"You know, when there's no watchtower or gallows in prospect, poets become bourgeois." It was Arkady Gorin who said this. A bottle of alcohol in his hand, he came to join me in the kitchen, and, as happens to men who are tipsy, we felt as if we were speaking with one voice, reading one another's thoughts, transmitting them through the telepathy that is such a distinctive feature of the glazed drunkenness of the small hours. "Once in the West, I'll be stricken with poetic impotence, you'll see . . . ," he added with a tragicomic sigh.

"So what are they up to over there?" I asked, interrupting him.

He might have understood me to mean: over there in the West. But, thanks to the alcohol, he knew I meant the people we had just walked away from.

"Over there, Chutov is reading the second part of his 'Kremlin Zoo.' But no one's listening, because your girlfriend's having another fuck behind the abstract art. With the American. He's using a pretty pale blue condom. They say that in the West they have rubbers that smell of fruit as well. Even taste of fruit. I wonder if the American . . . Oh, I'm sorry. I didn't mean to . . . Would you like me to go and smash this bottle over the fat imperialist shark's head? Fine . . . Well, let's go!"

And, when we were out in the street, he added: "The day after tomorrow I'll be in Vienna. But, you know, what I'm going to miss is the snow swirling around the lampposts. And the dirty streets. And the hallways in apartment blocks that smell of cat piss."

Suddenly he began shouting, waving his arms about and throwing his head back: "Oh happy day! I'm getting the hell out of here! I'm leaving this shitty country. I'm going to live in the West! I'll have dollar bills crackling in my sensitive intellectual's fingers! Bills greener than the tree of life. . . . I'm free! To hell with all the slaves who live around here!"

In fact, our two voices chimed as one, hurling abuse into the night. Mocking the dark windows in the apartment blocks, the sleep of all those "slaves" of the regime, cowards who did not dare to shout like us, giving full throat to their disgust. And who, by their resignation, reinforced the prison society in which we lived. They were our enemies. Drunk as we were that night in March, we believed this. It enabled us to forget our failures: in his case, a botched farewell to the Wigwam; in mine, the pattern of beauty spots on the legs of the woman I loved and had just lost.

We ran into these enemies of ours in the first local train heading for Leningrad. There they all were, a tightly packed crowd of them, undifferentiated, a sluggish mass of blank faces, bodies numb with lethargy, crudely dressed, with no scrap of imagination. These were not even the proletarians glorified by ideology, the "toiling masses" portrayed at every street corner on enormous propaganda posters. No, this was an underclass of humble cogs in the system: elderly women on their way to scrape up filth in smoke-filled factories with metal brooms, men on their way to load industrial trucks with rusty scrap or to trudge around concrete factory enclosures at thirty below, with ancient rifles on their shoulders. Creatures invisible in daylight hours who could only be observed in the still nocturnal darkness of a winter morning on this very first train of the day.

We remained standing, the better to observe them. Our aggressive bawling of a moment ago modulated into malevolent whispers. There before us, packed together on the benches, they formed a *tableau vivant* of what the regime could do to human beings: depriving them of all individuality, drilling them to the point where, of their own free will, they read *Pravda* (there were several papers open here and there), but, above all, cramming into their skulls the notion of their own contentment. For who among these somnolent cogs would have failed to perceive himself as happy?

"Just look at how drab they all look," snorted Arkady. "If the Germans invaded again, you could send them straight out to dig trenches. Or into the camps. They wouldn't even have to adjust."

"Into the camps?" I added, taking my tone from him. "They look as if they've just come out of them."

"And do you know what? If, instead of taking us to Leningrad, this terrible snail of a train turned and headed off toward Siberia, not one of them would dare ask why."

Suddenly we noticed this man's hands.

He was holding open a copy of *Pravda* by gripping it firmly between his thumbs and what was left of his hands, stumps from which all four fingers were missing.

I heard Arkady give a discreet cough and remark in a low, somewhat tremulous voice: "A machine-gunner . . . In the war, you know, they had those great machine guns, with shields that protected the head from shell splinters.

But the grip left the hands totally exposed. The steel only covered the thumb. So when there was a burst of shrapnel . . ."

The man turned the page very nimbly with his stumps.

We looked at the passengers' hands. They greatly resembled one another. Men's hands, women's hands, almost the same; heavy, the joints swollen from work, dark in hue from wrinkles stained with grease. Some of these hands clutched a book or newspaper, others, resting palm upward on knees, seemed, by their stillness, to be making a grave, simple statement. The faces, sometimes with closed eyes, also reflected this calm gravity.

The man with *Pravda* folded up his paper and, like a handicapped magician, stuffed it into his coat pocket. The train stopped, he got off.

"In the end, you know," murmured Arkady, "it's thanks to these people we can read out our rah-rah-rah-revolutionary poems and get laid using exotic fruit-flavored rubbers. Thanks to their wars. The fingers they lost . . ."

I made no reply, reflecting that among these elderly passengers there were doubtless some who in their youth had defended Leningrad during the siege. People under bombardment for more than two years, in freezing cold apartments, in streets dotted with corpses. And very likely working in the same factories they were still traveling to now. Accusing no one. Uncomplaining. I had always taken this resignation for a servility skillfully imposed by the regime. For the first time, in this suburban train, I thought I could discern something else in it.

The coach doors opened, the people went out into the snow-swept blackness, vanished into the shadow of long, dark brown brick walls.

As Leningrad drew nearer, the appearance of the passengers changed. Better dressed, younger, more talkative. Our contemporaries. The only person resembling those early travelers on the train was an old woman down in the subway looking lost, who quickly vanished at an intersection of the tunnels.

"You and I are going to get out," said Arkady. "To Boston or London. And in the end, you know, they'll be making perfumed rubbers here, too. But the old men with their fingers missing will have gone. And so much the better for them. I'm off tomorrow. If you've got any masterpieces that need shipping to the West . . ."

I received three letters from him, roughly five years apart, all from Israel; then, nine years later, a postcard from New York. The first letter announced the birth of his daughter. The second told me the child was learning the piano. The third (but his handwriting had greatly changed) said the girl had been injured in a bomb attack and had lost three fingers from her left hand. Learning of this, I would be reminded of the machine-gunner reading *Pravda*. Such is the stupid way with coincidences, always timed to demonstrate the inhuman absurdity of man's activities. I would also reflect on the monstrous mixture of happiness and heartbreak that must be experienced by parents when everyone regarded their child as having been spared.

The card from New York said: "If, fifteen years ago, I could have imagined what I've become today, I'd have hanged myself from the big pipe on the tank in the Wigwam shithouse. Do you remember that pipe where the rust had made a picture of Mephisto's head on the wall?"

In my own case, what that trickle of rust used to remind me of was a sailing ship with an incredibly tall mast.

When he left me in the subway at Leningrad, Arkady also proposed this job to me, a commitment he could no longer fulfill because of his departure: to go into the Archangel region, and write a series of reports on local habits and customs. "In the provinces, you know, they always want a graduate from Moscow or Leningrad. It's for their commemorative album. Some town anniversary or a folk festival. Whatever. You should go. Go and jot down a few fibs about the gnomes in their forests. But the main thing is, there'll be lots of material for your anti-Soviet satire. . . . I'll be off at the crack of dawn. Don't bother to come to the airport."

In August of that same year, I found myself in the village of Mirnoe, a few steps away from a woman who had just hauled in a fishing net. A woman waiting for the man she loved.

THAT DAY I RAN INTO HER AGAIN in the same place as the first time, in the willow plantation at the edge of the lake. The branches had already lost their leaves, the red clay along the shoreline was all streaked with this muted gold. Dressed in her old cavalry greatcoat and shod in heavy boots, she was pushing a boat silted up among the columns of rushes. A vessel too broad and heavy for rowing, designed no doubt for sailing. But perhaps the only one left in these parts that was still able to float.

"Can I help you?"

She stood up, smiled at me distractedly, as if through a glass dulled by memories, acquiesced.

After a few heaves, our bodies keeping time with one another, the boat slid into the water, at once becoming light, dancing. I held onto the gunwale to let Vera step on board, climbed in after her, tried to take an oar.

"I'll do it," she said softly. "There's too much wind. You need to know the ins and outs of it. Take her instead. . . ."

Her? Laid across the planks of the seat in the stern, I saw a long bundle in a thick cocoon of homespun cloth. Its shape indicated no particular contents but nevertheless gave rise to an obscure anxiety. I picked it up, astonished at its weight, looked at Vera, who was already propelling the boat far from the shore, against the wind.

"It's Anna," she explained to me. "She died three days ago. You'd gone to the district capital. . . ."

Anna, the old woman I had seen leaving the little *izba* bathhouse in Vera's company at the beginning of September.

I settled down, balanced the dead woman's body on my knees, clasping it clumsily, the way childless men do when someone hands them a baby.

The ultra-swift scudding of the clouds turned that day into a syncopated alternation of twilight and sunshine, springlike brilliance and autumnal relapse. When the sky grew leaden, I would become aware that I was hugging a corpse; then, amid the dazzle of the sunbeams, an irrational surge of hope would grip me: "No. What I hold in my arms is still of our world. Still inseparable from this sunlight, from the raw chill of the waves . . ."

Toward the center of the lake the swell became severe, the boat pitched, the foam began to whiten the exposed shoreline. I was clutching my burden tightly now, as I would have done with any other load. Vera pulled strongly on the oars, thrusting aside the gray water, which parted with the ponderousness of jelly. I watched this woman's body leaning forward, then flinging itself backward with legs stretched, chest and stomach to the fore, in a powerful physical thrust. Beneath the coarse fabric of her greatcoat, I glimpsed the delicate lace collar of a white blouse. . . . A wave struck the side with extra fury, and I was obliged to lift up the woman I held in my arms, hoist her close to my face, just as if, stricken with grief, I could not bear to be separated from a loved one.

It was during this crossing, which in the end lasted scarcely half an hour, that I began to have my first doubts about the real reason for my attachment to this northern village.

Within a few weeks I had realized that my quest for local customs and legends could just as well have been pursued in the libraries of Archangel. All the folklore of wedding and funeral rituals had long since been documented in books. Whereas on the spot, in these almost deserted villages, the memory of traditions was being lost, for want of any means of passing them on.

This forgetting of the past was all the more marked at Mirnoe, where the inhabitants were, so to speak, expatriates, elderly women driven from their homes by solitude, illness, the indifference of their families. Responding to my questions, they told touching tales of their own misfortunes. And of the war. For it was this that had erased all other legends from the popular memory. To these elderly inhabitants of Mirnoe, it was becoming the one remaining myth, a vivid and personal one, and one in which the immortals, both good and evil, were their own husbands and sons, the Germans, the Russian soldiers, Stalin, Hitler. And more specifically, the soldier Vera was waiting for.

As in all newly created myths, the roles of gods and devils were not yet set in stone. The Germans, the subject of visceral, passionate hatred, suddenly put in an appearance in the person of a sad-faced cook named Kurt. Zoya, a tall old woman who had the features of an icon darkened with age, had come across him in an occupied village near Leningrad, where she lived during the war. This German secretly brought remnants of food to the children of the village. . . . The place he had in local mythology was equal to that of a Hitler or a Zhukov.

In the end, I despaired of being able to record wedding choruses, songs in celebration of birth or death. The only ditty I heard on those old lips told of the departure of the local soldiers who had, it seemed, prevented the Nazi troops joining forces with Marshal Mannerheim's Finnish army. Thus the blockade of Leningrad had not become total. Provisions reached the besieged city via a corridor the men of this region had paved with their corpses. Were they all from this region? And Mirnoe? I doubted it. But when I looked at the old women of the village, I realized that this slim consolation was all they had left: the belief that, thanks to their husbands, brothers, or sons, Leningrad had not fallen.

Before coming to Mirnoe, I used to call such things "official propaganda." Such a description, I saw now, was a little on the terse side.

My idea of writing a satire also turned out to be easier said than done. I had envisaged portraying the grotesque system of kolkhozes, widespread drunkenness to the sound of loudspeakers broadcasting uplifting slogans. But these villages were quite simply abandoned or dying, reduced to a mode of survival not very different from the Stone Age. I managed to find a highly typical alcoholic, a character who would have lent himself very well to the humor of dissident prose. A house stripped bare by his drunken expenditure, his wife, still young, who looked twenty years older than she was and whose face bore a perpetual grimace of bitterness, his four silent children, resigned to living with this man who got down on all fours, vomiting and sobbing, and whom they had to call "Daddy."

I had almost completed the first page of my story when I learned that the drunkard had hanged himself. I had just arrived with Otar in the village where the suicide's family lived. The militia and the investigating magistrate were already there. The man had ended his life in a shed by fastening the rope to the door handle. He was almost squatting, his head thrown back, as if in a burst of coarse laughter. His children, whom nobody had thought of taking away, stared at him fixedly, without crying. His wife's face even seemed relaxed. The walls of the shed were hung with solid, old-fashioned tools, which inspired confidence despite the rust. Great tongs, heavy braces, iron contraptions whose names and functions had long been forgotten . . . One of the children suddenly backed away and began running across a broad fallow field bristling with yellowed plants.

No, this was not really material for a satirical story.

In this remote corner of the Russian North, I had expected to discover a microcosm of the Soviet age, a caricature of that simultaneously messianic and stagnant time. But time was completely absent from these villages, which seemed as if they were living on after the disappearance of the regime, after the collapse of the empire. What I was passing through was, in effect, a kind of premonition of the future. All trace of history had been eradicated. What remained were the gilded slivers of the willow leaves on the dark surface of the lake, the first snows that generally came at night, the silence of the White Sea, looming beyond the forests. What remained was this woman in a long military greatcoat, following the shoreline, stopping at the mailbox where the roads met. What remained was the essence of things.

During the first weeks of my life at Mirnoe, I did not dare to acknowledge it.

Then on a September afternoon crisscrossed with bursts of sunlight and brief spells of dusk, I found myself in a heavy craft, blackened with age, clasping a dead old woman in my arms, warming her with my body.

As the island drew near, the wind subsided and we landed on a sunlit beach, like summer but for the grass burned by the cold.

"In the old days they came here on foot. It wasn't an island, just a hill," Vera explained as she and I carried Anna's body. "But with no one to maintain the dikes anymore, the lake has doubled in size. They say that one day the sea will come right up to here. . . ."

Her voice struck me. A voice infinitely alone amid the watery expanse.

The sun, already low, its rays horizontal, made our presence seem unreal, as if echoing some secret objective. Our shadows stretched far across the churchyard studded with mounds, slanted up the flaking roughcast walls of the little church. Vera opened the door, disappeared, returned carrying a coffin. . . . The sides of the grave displayed a multitude of truncated roots. "Like so many lives cut short."

I said this to myself, for want of being able to make sense of what was taking place in front of me. A simple burial, of course. But also our silence, the great wind impaling itself on the church's cross, the utterly banal banging of the hammer. I was afraid Vera was going to ask me to nail down the coffin, the pathetic fear of missing, of knocking a nail in crooked . . . And as we lowered the coffin into the earth with the aid of ropes, this thought occurred: that dead woman, whom I warmed as I clasped her in my arms, is carrying a part of me away with her, but to where?

The return, with the wind behind us, was easy. A few strokes of the oars, which Vera repeated slowly, as if absentmindedly. Her body was in repose, and this repose reminded me, at one moment, of the relaxation of a body that has just given itself up to the act of love.

For a few weeks more, I would manage to convince myself that I was remaining in this northern land solely to gather some fragments of folklore. "Besides, at Mirnoe, I'm onto a good thing," I told myself. "No rent to pay. Half the houses are unoccupied. You move in. You make yourself at home. This is real communism!"

Mirnoe time, that floating, suspended time, gradually absorbed me. I melted into the imperceptible flow of autumn light, a duration with no other objective than the tarnished gold of the leaves, the fragile lace of early morning hoarfrost on the rim of a well, the fall of an apple from a bare branch in a silence so limpid you could hear the rustle of the grass beneath the fallen fruit.

In this life forgotten by time, all was simultaneously weighty and light. Anna's burial. This day, funereal and yet marked by an airy luminosity, a new serenity. Beside her grave that other cross, the name of a certain Vassily Drozd and the uneven inscription, cut with a knife: "A good man." Around this "good man" a dotted line of chamomile flowers, sheltered from the wind by the earth of the grave. And Vera's voice, saying very simply: "Next time I'll bring her cross for her."

Often, when I saw her leaving Mirnoe or returning, I would repeat: "There goes a woman who has waited thirty years. . . ." But the tones of tragedy and despair with which I invested these words failed to make them conclusive. Almost every morning, Vera went off to the school where she taught on the other side of the lake. She generally walked around along the shore, but when the floods cut off the paths, I sometimes saw her getting into the old boat. Following her with my eyes, I would say to myself: "A woman who has turned her life into an infinity of waiting. . . ." I would feel a moment of inner vertigo for a time, but not the alarm I anticipated.

Besides, nothing unusual about Vera gave any sign of this appalling wait. "There are a great many single women, here or elsewhere, when all is said and done," was the only argument I could find to justify the commonplace way it was possible to think about this whole life being sacrificed. "Lots of single women who, out of courage or modesty, make no display of their grief. Women very much like Vera, give or take a few years of waiting . . ."

Even the mailbox at the crossroads gradually lost its significance in my eyes as a killer of hope. Zoya, the doughtiest of the old women, was the one who most often went to collect the mail. The others readied themselves for her trips there and back, as for long pilgrimages, waiting for her as if every one of them were bound to receive a letter. Generally, nothing. Occasionally a card addressed to the one who was no longer there . . . When I met Zoya on one of her postal excursions, I would ask her to bring me back a nice love letter. She would give me a mischievous smile and proclaim: "It'll be coming soon. They're cutting down the tree to make paper for your letter. You'll just have to be patient!" She would continue on her way and return an hour later with the local newspaper folded under her arm. Occasionally I read it: even this news, geographically so close to Mirnoe, seemed as if it came from another world, from an era where time existed.

THE NEAREST TOWN where time did still follow its course was the district capital. I made the acquaintance of a group of the local intelligentsia there: the deputy director of the cultural center, the young librarian in charge of the municipal library, the surgeon from the hospital, a nurse, two teachers (art and history), the reporter from the newspaper *Lenin's Path,* and some others.

I was both surprised and not to discover that they had their own "Wigwam," their dissident group that met in the deputy director's big *izba.* The same rejection of the regime animated their discussions. But if our targets in Leningrad had mainly been the Kremlin Zoo and its dinosaurs, here the monsters to be slain were the secretary of the local Party committee and the editor-in-chief of *Lenin's Path.* In their well-lubricated late-night debates the latter used to be compared to Goebbels. . . .

The standing accorded to me was enviable in the extreme: I came from the country's intellectual capital, the only truly European city in the empire, and was thus a virtual westerner. My role at their soirées resembled that of the American journalist at our Leningrad Wigwam. Here what all their displays of dissidence and amorousness sought was my approval. Once, when the reporter was busily comparing his editor-in-chief to Goebbels, the mischievous thought occurred to me that it was a real shame I had no condoms with exotic fruit flavors to offer them.

I was a westerner of straw.

During the last days of September, I would prepare each evening to leave Mirnoe the following morning. But I stayed. I convinced myself I must definitely witness a certain marriage ritual the old women had promised to enact one day. "It's a shame Anna's no longer with us," they said. "She was our soloist. We only know the choruses." The ritual, strictly local to the region according to them, was simple. The bridegroom carried his chosen one up to the hill where the church stood, in a light cart if the causeway to the island was fordable, in a boat if the meadows were flooded. Sole master of the reins or the oars on the way out, on the way back he invited his young bride to share his task. "I can't leave until I've heard the song that goes with this." Such was the excuse I frequently gave myself.

Right up to that day, perhaps. A day of thick fog, the dull silhouette of a woman, upright in a boat. Vera, returning to the village. I grasped the end of the long oar she held out to me, helped her to heave the bows onto the clay of the shore. And noticed that, amid the freezing mist enveloping us, the wood of the oar had retained the warmth of her hands. I had never yet felt so close to this woman.

The next day, still in the cotton-wool blindness of the fog, Otar, from whom I had hitched a ride on the road out of the district capital, lost his way. He was trying to show me an abandoned village with a wooden church, and once we left the main road we found ourselves in dense, ragged whiteness, from which a branch shot out at intervals to lash the windshield. The wheels of the truck skidded and spun, digging deeper and deeper ruts from which the mud spurted. We turned, backed, advanced tentatively, but everywhere the ground seemed to consist of the same peat, sodden with water. The trees loomed up in front of us with the stubbornness of ghosts in a dream.

In the end Otar switched off the engine, got out,

disappeared, returned after a minute: "No good. In a pea-soup fog like this it's best to stay put. I was only a couple of yards away, and I couldn't even see the truck. Let's have a drink instead. And wait. This evening there'll be a wind. . . ."

To begin with we drank half a bottle of vodka he kept under his seat, then a bottle of Georgian wine. "Only because you're a good listener," he explained. Dusk tinted the fog blue, and the growing darkness harmonized pleasantly with our drunken state. As was his wont, Otar talked about women, but was interrupted by the cautious, snuffling appearance of four wild boars: a mother and her three little ones. Also lost, no doubt, in this freezing whiteness. They sniffed at the wheels of the truck, then scuttled away, pursued by roars of laughter from us.

"On the subject of pigs," remarked Otar, "I know a good one. A real pig of a story! There's a Russian, a Georgian, and an Azerbaijani going back to their village in the morning after a hell of a night on the town. And suddenly a big fat sow crosses the road in front of them and runs off. It tries to get through a hole in the fence, but its great ass gets stuck there. It wriggles and squeals, and twirls its tail. The Russian looks at this fat rear end and says: 'Oh my! If only it was Sophia Loren!' Then the Georgian sighs: 'Oh my! If only it was my neighbor's wife!' And the Azerbaijani licks his lips and groans: 'Oh my. If only it was dark out!' Ha! Ha! Ha!"

We laughed loudly enough to frighten all the wild boars in the forest, then, when calm had returned, Otar maintained silence for a long while, with the insight of a drunken man suddenly sensing that something in his merriment does not ring true, turning melancholy, brooding on a lifetime's sorrows laid bare.

The fog cleared. A hundred yards from the thickets where we had allowed ourselves to get trapped, the cross-roads came into view, the post with the mailbox, and above it the little sign with the name: Mirnoe. By the light of the setting sun, still made hazy by strands of mist, the inscription seemed to be emerging from nothingness, like a signpost amid the debris of an abandoned planet.

I was just about to climb down when Otar began speaking in a low, sad voice that was quite unlike him: "I want to give you a piece of advice. You're young. It may be of use to you. When it comes to love, you want to act like that fat pig of an Azerbaijani. That's right. So as not to get hurt, you need to be a filthy swine. You see a female, you fuck her, you move on to the next one. Whatever you do, steer clear of love! I tried it, and it got me six years in a camp. She was the one, my goddamned sweetheart, may she rot in hell, who squealed on me. She was the one who reported my skins and furs business. Six years in a camp and four years' probation up here in this dump. Ten years of my life wiped out. I've had enough. With women, I'm a pig because they're all sows. You get to stick it in, you screw her, and: next!"

He fell silent, then smiled bitterly. "You're an artist. You need beauty and tenderness. But never forget this: all women are sows stuck in a hole in a fence. And the ones who aren't are the ones that suffer. Like her . . . like Vera."

He drove off in a flurry; the water stirred in the ruts, then came to rest, reflecting the blaze of the sunset.

In the distance, beneath the tall pivotal beam of a well, I saw Vera. Long trails of fog, the scarlet rays of the low sun, deep stillness, and this woman, such a stranger to all the words that had just been spoken.

So perhaps what kept me in Mirnoe was this feeling of strangeness I had never before experienced as intensely. In this aftertime where the village lived, it was as if things and people were liberated from their uses and were starting to be loved simply for their presence beneath the northern sky.

What was the use of that wild-mushroom-gathering trip we embarked on one day, Vera and I? Without conferring or planning, the way everything happened here. We knew the harvest would not amount to more than a few boleti pockmarked by the frosts, a dozen or so russulas, fragile as glass. In this forest, already half stripped of its leaves, we walked beside one another, speaking little, often forgetting how to search properly. And when we remembered that you have to part the bracken, turn over the dead leaves, we did it overzealously, like two lazybones caught red-handed. During these frenzied bouts we lost sight of each other, and I would be intensely aware of this woman getting farther away and then, after the snapping of a twig, of our drawing closer again. Sometimes Vera appeared soundlessly, catching me off guard, immersed as I was in the slow filtering of rustlings and silences. Occasionally, it was I who surprised her, all alone amid the trees. Then I felt like a wild animal coolly observing a defenseless prey. She would turn and for a moment seem not to see me, or to be seeing someone other than me. And we would resume our wandering with a sense of not having dared an exchange of confidences.

If the truth be told, the point of this meandering stroll was seeing the long cavalry greatcoat that Vera wore, its coarse fabric patterned with tiny red and yellow leaves. Seeing her eyes, after a moment of forgetfulness, beginning to respond to my look. Hearing her voice: "That path would take you all the way to the sea. Possibly five or six hours' march. If we left now, we'd reach the coast close to midnight. . . ."

The point of this life apart from time was picturing our arrival on the shores of the White Sea in the middle of the night.

Or that evening, too, after my return with Otar, on the day he had talked about "pigs" and "sows." A very thin layer of ice had formed at the bottom of the well. (I had just caught up with Vera, who was drawing water.) As the ice broke, it sounded like a harpsichord. We looked at one another. We were each about to remark on the beauty of this tinkling sound, then thought better of it. The resonance of the harpsichord had faded into the radiance of the air, it blended with the wistfully repeated notes of an oriole, with the scent of a wood fire coming from the nearby *izba*. The beauty of that moment was quite simply becoming our life.

There was that alder tree as well, the last to keep its immense helmet of bronze foliage intact. It overhung the shore at the place where Vera generally landed. As we moved across the water we would see it from afar, this swaying pyramid freighted with gold, and kept an eye on it as the last island of summer, holding out against the bareness of autumn.

And then one morning two clouds of misty breath from our double "Oh!" faded upon the air. Every leaf, down to the last tiny bronze roundel, had fallen during the night. The black branches, stripped bare, carved into the stinging blue of the sky like fissures. We drew close to one another, contriving to hold back obvious remarks ("It was too lovely to last"). And then, as we walked down to the shore, saw, reproduced in the copper-colored glory of the leaves on the water, the inlaid pattern that had tumbled out of the sky. The dark, smooth water, this red-and-gold incrustation. An even broader mosaic, one slowly spreading beneath the breeze, becoming an up-turned canopy, ready to cover the whole lake. The eye was swept along by its endless expansion. Another beauty was being re-created, new and strange, richer than before, even more alive after its autumnal death.

Thus it was that in the language I employed in those days, I made a record of such luminous moments rescued from time. I sensed that they were not just harmonious fragments but a complete life apart. The one I had always dreamed of giving expression to. It was this I had had in mind in front of the broken skylight at the Wigwam. Here in Mirnoe, such a life could be lived from day to day with the certainty that it was exactly the life one should always have been living.

In these notes, jotted down between drafts of satirical prose and the details of rituals and legends, I was trying to hold on to it.

In the same notebook this fragment, written one

evening: "During the night a violent gale drove the boat into the middle of the lake. The roads are impassable, so to get to the school Vera has to wait and hope that the wind coming off the sea will bring the boat in again. The breeze stiffens, we see our skiff drifting slowly toward us. Elsewhere a wait like this would seem intolerable to me, here this piece of floating wood marks out a span of time made up of sunshine, bitter cold, and a woman's voice, weaving itself into the air in rare words like the stray chords of a melody. And the fragments of ice we break off at the frozen margin of the lake. Intricate rose windows of hoarfrost: we amuse ourselves by looking through them at the sky, the lake, and one another, transformed by these fans of crystal. The ice melts, shatters in our fingers, but the vision of the world transfigured stays in our eyes for a few more seconds. At one moment, a rustling in the willow groves at the water's edge surprises us: driven by the wind from the White Sea, the boat has just reached the shore. We had not noticed time passing."

On occasion I would say to myself, firmly believing it: "She's a woman who lives by these rare moments of beauty. What more could she offer the one she loves?" In a confused intuition, I then grasped that, for Vera, experiencing them was a way of communicating with the man she was waiting for.

THAT NIGHT I HAD JUST BEEN RECORDING the episode with the boat in my notebook.

All at once a dull sound detached itself from the limpid stillness of midnight, the slamming of a door a long way off. I went out and just had time to see briefly illuminated the entrance to the little bathhouse *izba,* on the slope that led to the lake. The door closed, but the darkness was not total. Under a milky blue, the hazy moon was keeping a wary, phosphorescent watch over the houses and trees. It was strangely mild; not a breath of wind blew down the village street. The dust on the road was silvery and soft underfoot.

I started to walk, not knowing where I was going. At first it was probably a simple urge to melt into this cloudy, somewhat theatrical luminescence, one that made every enchantment, every evil spell possible. But very soon, with a sleepwalker's persistence, I found myself close to the bathhouse.

The tiny window, two hands wide, was tinged with a lemon-colored halo, certainly a candle. The smell of burned bark hung on the air, mingling with the pungent chill of the rushes and the wet clay of the lakeshore. A mild night, a respite before the onslaught of winter. A feeling that my presence here was utterly uncalled-for and quite essential for something unknowable. The ideas that came to mind were crude, incongruous: to draw close to the little window, spy on this woman as she soaped her body, or quite simply, to throw open the door, step up to her, embrace her slippery, elusive body, push her down onto the wet floorboards, possess her. . . .

The recollection of what this woman was interrupted my delirium. I recalled the day when the wind had carried the boat away, the fragments of ice through which we had peered at the sky, Vera's face, made iridescent by the cracks in the rime, her faint smile, her gaze returning mine through the ice jewels as they melted between her fingers. This woman was situated beyond all desire. The woman waiting for the man she loved.

At that moment, the door opened. The woman who emerged was naked: she stepped out of the steam room, stood on the little wooden front steps, and inhaled the cool of the lake. The soft radiance of the moon made of her a statue of bluish glass, revealing even the molding of collarbones, the roundness of breasts, the curve of hips, on which drops of water glistened. She did not see me; a woodpile concealed me in its angular shadow. Besides, her eyes were half closed, as if all she perceived came through the sense of smell, from animal instinct. She breathed in greedily, baring her body to the moon, offering it to the night, to the dark expanse of the lake.

In the face of this dazzling, naked, physical presence, all I had thought about this woman hitherto, all I had written about her life, seemed trifling. A body capable of giving itself, of taking pleasure, directly, naturally. Nothing stood in the way of this, apart from that ancient, almost mythical vow: the wait for the vanished soldier. A ghost from the past versus a woman ready to love and be loved. Not even to love, no, just to yield to carnal abandon. In the silence of the night I heard her breathing, I sensed the quivering of her nostrils—a she-wolf or a hind, sniffing the scents rising from the water's edge. . . . She turned her back, and in the moment before she disappeared inside the door, the moonlight picked out the firm, muscular play of her buttocks.

Next morning, on a confused impulse of desire, I once

more followed the path to the bathhouse. I looked back often, afraid of revealing my intentions, which I could not explain even to myself. The inside of the little building, darkened by smoke over long years, seemed chilly, sad. On the narrow ledge beside the tiny window, the melted lump of a candle. In the corner, close to the stove, dominating the room, a great cast-iron bowl rested in the hollow of a pyramid of sooty stones. A little water at the bottom of a copper scoop. An acid smell of damp wood. Impossible to imagine the heat of the fire, the stifling steam, a burning hot female body, writhing amid this blissful inferno. . . . Then, suddenly, this slender, worn ring. Left behind on a bench beneath the window!

I slipped away, imagining how by a hideous coincidence, typical of such situations, Vera might come back looking for it and see me here. This ring alone made the nocturnal vision an undeniable reality. Yes, that woman had been here. A woman with a body made for pleasure and love, a woman whose only desire, perhaps, was just this, a sign, a slight pressure from circumstances, to liberate her from her absurd vow. The ring she had taken off was more telling than all the speculations I had set down in my notebook.

I was certain I should be adding nothing further now to my notes on Vera's life.

Two days later, I was writing: "The villagers who long ago abandoned their houses at Mirnoe carried away everything it was possible to carry. The seat of the village administration (an *izba* hardly larger than the others) was emptied as well. They tried to remove a large mirror, a relic of the era before the revolution. Through bad luck or clumsiness, hardly had it been set down on the front steps when it snapped, a long crack that split it in two. Rendered useless, it was left behind, propped against the timbers of the house. Its upper portion reflects the forest treetops and the sky. The face of anyone looking into it is thrust up toward the clouds. The lower part reflects the rutted road, the feet of people walking past, and, if you glance sideways, the line of the lake, now blue, now dark. . . . That evening I chance upon Vera in front of the mirror. She remains motionless, slightly bowed over the tarnished glass. When she hears my footsteps and looks around, what I see distinctly in her eyes is a day very different from the one we are living in at present, a different sky and, in my place, another person. Refocusing her look, she recognizes me, greets me, we walk away in silence. . . . All my overheated portrayals of the naked woman on the steps of the bathhouse are absurd. Her life is truly and solely made up of these moments of grievous beauty."

I noticed that certain of the old women of Mirnoe, as they walked past the great abandoned mirror, would sometimes stop, take a handkerchief, and wipe the rain-streaked glass.

It was after our encounter beside the broken mirror that I found myself tempted to try to understand how it was to spend one's whole life waiting for someone.

TWO

I

ONLY TWO MOMENTS IN THAT LIFE were known to me, and yet they encompassed it in its entirety.

The first: a dull, mild April day, a girl of sixteen shuffling in wet snow. Her eyes follow a convoy of four broad sleighs sliding over the slushy, gray potholes of the thaw like flat-bottomed boats. Amid the throng of young conscripts' laughing faces, this sad pair of eyes she is trying not to lose sight of. She quickens her pace, slips, the eyes disappear behind someone's shoulder, then reappear, glimpsing her amid the great emptiness of the snow-covered fields.

It is the beginning of April 1945, the very last contingent to be sent to the front and, on the last sleigh, this young soldier, the man she loves, the man to whom, as they said good-bye, she swore something like eternal love, something childish, I tell myself, yes, swore to be utterly true to him or to wait until death. I have no idea what a woman in love for the first time may promise a man, I have never received such a promise, I have never believed a woman capable of keeping it. . . . The convoy turns off behind the forest, the girl continues walking. The air has the wild smell of spring, of horses, of freedom. She stops, looks. Everything is familiar. This crossroads, the lake, the darkness of the forest where the bark is swollen with water. Everything is unrecognizable. And filled with life. A new life. Suddenly, from a very long way off, a cry goes up, holds, for an instant, in the dusk over the plain, fades. The girl listens: " . . . I'll be back," yelled at the top of his lungs, becomes first an echo, then silence, then an inner resonance that will never leave her.

That first moment I pictured thanks to the stories told by the old women of Mirnoe. The second I witnessed for myself: a woman of forty-seven walking beside the lake on a clear, cold September evening, the same path taken for thirty years, the same serene look directed at a passerby, and in her reverie that voice still resounds with unaltered power: ". . . I'll be back!"

Between those two moments in her life, between her promise made in youth and the future annihilated by this vow, I tried to conjure up the day when the balance had tilted, when a few hasty words, whispered amid the tears of parting, had become her fate.

The tragedy of her life, I told myself, had come into being almost by chance. The random sequence effect of the tiny facts of daily life, apparently harmless coincidences, the overlapping of dates that, to begin with, presaged nothing irremediable. The subtle mechanism that sets all the real dramas of our lives in motion.

In April 1945, when the man she loved went to the front, she was sixteen.

So this was her first love, no capacity there for seeing things in perspective, making of this love one of the loves of her life. If the man had been killed at the start of the war, if she had been older, if she had been in love before, it would all have turned out differently. But on the day he went away, Berlin was about to fall, and this young man's death at the age of eighteen seemed brutally gratuitous and quite easily avoidable. Give or take a few days and one less battle he would have returned, life would have resumed its course in May: marriage, children, the smell of resin on fresh pine planks, clean linen flapping in the wind that blew from the White Sea. If only . . .

I knew that writers had long since used up all of these "if onlys" in books, in film scenarios. In Russia, in Germany.

During the postwar years, the two countries, the one victorious, the other defeated, had been hell-bent on writing and rewriting the same scene: a soldier returns to the town of his birth and discovers his wife or his beloved happy as a lark in the arms of another. The age-old Colonel Chabert triangle . . . In some versions, the soldier would return disfigured and therefore be rejected. In some, he would learn of a betrayal and forgive. In some, he would not forgive. In some, she would wait, then could wait no longer, and he would appear just as she was about to remarry. Every one of these moral quandaries went hand in hand with agonizing "if onlys," which was, after all, not inappropriate, given the number of couples rent asunder and loves left to wither on the vine in both countries, thanks to the war.

It was via literature of this kind that I had sought to understand Vera's life, to weigh the "if onlys" that might have changed everything. But this unbelievable wait of thirty years (I was a mere twenty-six myself) struck me as too monstrous, too unarguable, to give rise to any moral debate. And, above all, much too improbable to feature in a book. A period of waiting far too long, too grievously real, for any work of fiction.

The bald reality of it was clear to me, too, in the obscenely simple manner of this life's devastation, the unspeakable banality of the years that had gone to make up that thirty-year monolith. For to begin with, when peace returned, there was nothing to distinguish Vera from the millions of other women who had lost their men. Like her they waited, young widows, forsaken lovers. No particular merit in that. Such waiting was very common then, and their distress was equally current.

Indeed, to probe the depths of her misfortune I had to face up to a still more brutal, almost indecent statement of fact: during those first few years without war, women remained faithful to their men who had been killed because there was a shortage of men left alive. It was as crass and prosaic as that. Ten million males slaughtered, as many again disabled. A fiancé became a rare commodity.

A hideous logic, but fearsomely accurate, I knew. The only one that enabled me to picture the village of Mirnoe as it had been thirty years before. A strange population made up of women, children, and old men. A few men sporting military medals on their soldiers' tunics, embittered men with arms missing, drink-sodden men with no legs, the heroic flotsam and jetsam of the victory. And this girl, this Vera, whose faithfulness at first passed unnoticed, later prompted respectful and sympathetic approval, then, as time went by, a mixture of weariness and irritation, the shrugging of shoulders reserved for village idiots; then, later still, indifference, sometimes giving way to the pride local people take in one of the curiosities of the region, a holy relic, a notably picturesque rock.

One day, in the end, nothing remained of all that. Just the beautiful emptiness of the clear September sky, this same faithful woman, thirty years older, steering a boat across the sun-drenched mirror of the lake. The way I had seen and known her. The pointlessness of all judgments, admiring or critical. Only this thought, hazy amid the air's radiance: "That's how it is."

It was more from a desire for the truth than youthful cynicism that I sought to strip her life of all will to sacrifice, all grand gestures. Vera had never really had a choice. The pressure of events, which is the destiny of the poor, had decided for her. At first the lack of men to marry, and then, when marriages began to be celebrated once more in the resurgent village, she was already perceived as a kind of young old maid. There was a new generation of truly young people, careless of the ghosts of the war, eager to seize their portion of happiness, wary of this solitary woman, half-widow, half-fiancée, dressed in a long cavalry greatcoat. Their zest for life had thrust her back toward old age as the draft from a train thrusts aside someone who has just missed it.

Impossible, too, for her to leave Mirnoe, a place in the back of beyond! In those days, kolkhozniks had no identity documents and needed to request authorization to travel. It was not the echo of a voice from beyond the forest that kept her there, but this bureaucratic slavery. And when, at the start of the sixties, Stalin's serfs, freed at last, were beginning to leave their warrens, Vera was already surrounded by a colony of moribund old women she could no longer abandon.

No, she had not chosen to wait, she had been cruelly caught by an era, by the postwar years, which had closed in on her like a mousetrap.

But this meant she was perfectly free! And her pledge was null and void.

Free to leave the village, as she did one day of high winds at the beginning of October. I noticed she was carrying not her leather bookbag crammed with textbooks and pupils' homework but a broad portfolio of thick cardboard, which the squalls were trying to snatch from her. There was a vagabond lightness in her step, the panache of an itinerant artist or an adventuress. As she passed the mailbox where the roads met, she did not pause. For the space of a second, the notion came to me that she was departing for good on an arrogant impulse. Off to take the train to Leningrad, or at least, to Archangel . . .

She was free. And her *mater dolorosa* persona was other people's invention. We were the ones who imposed this absurd waiting on her, very noble, of course, even heroic, but she would have shaken it off long ago had not our sympathetic and admiring gaze been fixed on her. This gaze had turned her into a pillar of salt, an elegant funeral monument, at the foot of which one could say a little prayer, sighing: "Praise be! Faithful women still exist!" The lovesick babbling of a sixteen-year-old girl had been turned into an irrevocable vow. And a woman brimming with vitality turned into a suttee burned to a cinder on the pyre of loneliness.

These judgments were exaggerated and too intellectual, but, in a confused way, I sensed that they should be made known to Vera at any cost. She ought to know it was possible to think in this way, that there was still time for such thoughts.

She came home that evening, with the same portfolio under her arm. "Leningrad, Archangel . . . hmm . . . ," I kept repeating bitterly. And yet, despite that false start, amid the wind's bluster, the sense of freedom that emanated from here appearance was still there. Even more intensely. And my indignation became still sharper over this cult of undying love that had been assigned to her, as to an idol. Here was a woman, her face flushed by the wind, walking along in the sunset's radiance. Everything else should be wiped from the slate, the youthful promises, the faded icons of past heroism, the pitying glances of kindly souls. Look no further than this free flesh-and-blood presence. As I watched her walking away, I recalled the body of a woman hauling in her nets on the warm clay of the lakeshore, and that naked body at night, in front of the door to the little bathhouse *izba*. . . . I sensed that the recovery of her freedom must start from the revolt of that body enclosed in a long military greatcoat.

I called on her that same evening, without being invited, simply knocking on her door on the pretext that I had run out of bread. I had been into her house before on several occasions, but always after meeting her in the street and exchanging a few words with her. This unannounced arrival did not surprise her, however; she was accustomed to life in a community and to the visits, always unexpected, of her elderly protégées.

We went into the main room, and while she was taking out a round loaf and cutting a generous quarter off it for me, I quickly seated myself in the place that was the secret goal of my visit. Alongside the old table of thick, cracked planks stood this bench, the far end of which, close to the door, was the spot Vera generally occupied when one went to see her. She talked, served her guests, walked over to the stove, but always returned to that station close to the door. At the least creak of the treads on the front steps, she would tense instinctively, ready to stand up, and go to meet the visitor who was surely bound to arrive at that very moment. And outside the window, she could see the crossroads, the corner of the forest that anyone coming to Mirnoe had to skirt. . . .

So I sat down at this end of the bench, leaning my elbows heavily on the table. Vera had wrapped my share of the loaf in a square of linen, then offered me tea and apple jam. She moved away, and I had a distinct feeling that the room's familiar disposition was eluding her. There were brief tremors of anxiety in her eyes and a slight uncertainty in the movements of her body, the alarm of a sleepwalker who has been diverted from her path. She poured tea for us, then, after some hesitation, settled herself on a chair facing me, stood up almost at once, crossed over to the window. I perceived that an unacknowledged, pleasurably cruel game was developing between us. . . . More or less honestly, I still believed it was for her own good.

I went back to her house three evenings in a row, always unexpectedly, each time settling myself down without permission on the very end of the bench close to the door. Her thwarted sleepwalker's body seemed to be accepting my intrusion better and better. Very remotely in our confrontation there was the tension of a sexual encounter.

Or rather that of a physical assault, for my presence distorted the interior of this room, prepared for another's return. The cleanliness of the floor, half a dozen reproductions on the walls and these books she had certainly never read (a pretentiousness that struck me as truly provincial and touching). Fat books lined up on a set of shelves, chosen to create "an intellectual ambience": a *General Theory of Linguistics,* an *Etymological Dictionary* in four volumes, Humboldt's *Complete Works* . . . They were clearly relics she had salvaged from some abandoned library, having no need of them for her own modest work as a teacher. . . . I settled myself down on the seat I had annexed, observing with curiosity this haven created for another: the order, the comfort, the bookish decor.

On the last of these games-playing evenings I interrupted my psychological experiment for a moment, glanced out of the window. And through the pallor of the fog I thought I could make out the tall figure of a man emerging at the crossroads. A traveler slowing his pace . . . No, nothing. A tree. A streak on the windowpane. But, viewed from this end of the bench, such an apparition seemed far from impossible, nurtured to the point of hallucination by years of waiting, by all those glances (it made me giddy to think of them) day after day, conjuring up a human shape suddenly visible at the corner of the forest. . . .

When I got home, I decided to leave Mirnoe the following morning.

Instead of leaving that morning, I went to the island with Vera.

SHE WAS DUE TO GO TO THE ISLAND to lay a wreath of dried flowers on Anna's grave—a pale ring, bristling with plant stems and ears of corn, which it had taken one of the old women of Mirnoe several weeks to fashion.

For me, crossing the lake in the rain perfectly expressed the absurdity of the existence Vera was leading. Absurd, too, was my own impulse to go with her, which took me by surprise: I was busy packing my bags, saw her passing in the street, opened the window, called out to her, asking, I did not know why, if I could join her. And to crown my folly, with ridiculous male conceit, I insisted on sculling with a single oar, standing upright, like an operatic gondolier. Vera began by objecting (the wind, the wayward heaviness of the old rowing boat . . .), then let me go ahead.

The wind kept shifting, the nose of the boat swung to the right, to the left, then came to a standstill, impossible to drive forward through the dense water, in which the oar became embedded, as if in wet cotton wool. So as not to lose face, I made light of it, concealed the effort, my arms soon numb, my brow furrowed, my eyes clouded with sweat. The woman seated in front of me, with the ugly, dry little wreath in her lap, was intolerable to behold—idiotically resigned, indifferent to the rain, to the wind, to her ruined life, to this day wasted on an expedition prompted by the funereal whim of some half-mad old woman. I contemplated her bowed face, brooding on dreams, faded, one supposed, by dint of recurring every day for thirty years, a reverie, or perhaps just a void, gray, monotonous as this water and these shores, blurred in the raindrop-laden air. "A woman they have turned into a walking monument to the dead. A fiancée immolated on the pyre of faithfulness. A rustic Andromache . . ." As my efforts became more painful, so the epithets became more venomous. At one point, it seemed to me as if the boat, mired in the glutinous ponderousness of the waves, were making no progress at all. Vera gently raised her face, smiled at me, seemed about to speak, changed her mind. "A village idiot! That's it! A wooden idol these yokels have nailed up at the entrance to their settlement to ward off fate's thunderbolts. A propitiatory victim offered to History. An icon in whose shadow the good old kolkhozniks could fornicate, indulge in denouncing people, steal, get drunk . . ."

Exhausted by struggling against the wind, I ended up heaving on the oar more or less mechanically, merely going through the motions, for form's sake. The squat outline of the church on the island hillock continued to appear as distant as ever. "Mind you, they still had to let her leave the village, poor Vera, for as long as it took for her to get her teaching diploma in some little town in the area. Doubtless the one great journey in her life. Her view into the world. And then, presto, back into the fold, her vigil on the bench by the front door, forever pricking up her ears. What if that's the sound of a soldier's boots? Oh yes, a little withered wreath for Anna's grave. Very pretty, my dear, but who's going to put flowers on your grave? The old women will die, and there won't be another Vera to take care of you. . . ."

I noticed that by matching my efforts to the thrust of the swell, I was maneuvering the boat more easily. It still moved heavily, but instead of battling against this massive pitching and tossing, one had to make a swift stroke with the oar at the right moment, give it a brief flick. . . . Vera remained unmoving and more detached than ever, as if, having noted that I had learned the technique, she could return to her reverie. She was shielding the flowers on the wreath with her hands. I wanted to say to her: "Look, the rain's going to drench them on the grave, in any case." But that would have disturbed her repose.

Well, why not rouse her? Stop sculling, squat down in front of her, clasp her hands, shake them, or better still, kiss her frozen hands. "She's asleep in a kind of foretaste of death, in that time she put on hold at the age of sixteen, moving like a somnambulist among these old women who remind her of the war and the departure of her soldier. . . . She's living in an afterlife. The dead must see what she sees. . . ."

We grounded gently on the island's beach. I jumped ashore, pulled the bow up onto the sand, helped Vera disembark. Suddenly, the idea that this woman was living through what it is only given to us to live through after we die made an obscure sense of the life I had judged so absurd. A sense that could be perceived at every step, in every gesture.

"I'm sorry to have made you work like a galley slave," she said as we walked up to the churchyard. "I could have hidden this at home, of course, or thrown it away" (she shook the wreath gently). "Zina would never have known. But, you see, all these old women are already living a little beyond this life, and I feel as if I'm reaching out to them across the frontier. Then all of a sudden they hand me this wreath. So maybe it's not so stupid, after all. . . . " She looked at me for a long time; her gray eyes seemed bigger than ever as they glistened in the rain, giving the impression that they had read my recent thoughts about her. I had a very physical sense that I, too, was present in this afterlife through which she was moving.

Once the wreath was placed on the grave mound, the flowers on it were quickly covered in raindrops and, moistened, seemed to come to life again like a delicate and luminous decal. "Next time I'll bring the cross," she said very softly, as if to herself. "May I come with you?" I asked, picturing a rainy day, the slow rocking of the boat, and the hand, currently adjusting the wreath, resting, as if forgotten, on the gunwale of the boat.

We began to walk down toward the shore. Vera's long military greatcoat was soaked through, almost black. At a distance, on this slope with its brown, flattened vegetation, she might have been taken for a nurse in wartime, making her way toward a field covered in the wounded and dead . . . In other people's eyes . . . But all I saw was a woman walking at my side, her face drenched by the rain, intensely alive on this dull autumn day, taking care not to tread on the last clumps of flowers, and as she arrived at the beach, bending down to pick something off the sand and hand it to me: "You dropped this last time." It was the pencil I had used to set down such phrases in my notebook as: "A suttee burned to a cinder on the pyre of faithfulness," "a life massacred by a childish vow" . . .

In the boat she took one oar, leaving the other for me. The rain fell more steadily, subduing the squalls. Neither the houses of Mirnoe, nor even the willows on that far shore, were visible. Our rhythms were quickly matched. Each effort made by the other felt like a response to one's own, down to the slightest tensing of the muscles. We touched shoulders, but our real closeness was in this slow, rhythmic action, the care we took to wait for each other, pulling together once more after too powerful a stroke or the skipping of a blade over the crest of a wave.

In the middle of the crossing, both shores disappeared completely behind the rain. No line, no point of orientation beyond the contours of the boat. The gray air with its swirling pattern of raindrops, the waves, calmer now, that seemed to be coming from nowhere. And our forward motion that no longer seemed to have a goal. We were quite simply there, side by side, amid the somnolent hissing of the rain, in a dusk as cool as fish scales, and when I turned my head a little I saw the glistening face of a woman smiling faintly, as if made happy by the incessant tears the sky sent coursing down her cheeks.

I understood now that this was the way she lived out her afterlife. A slow progress, with no apparent goal, but marked by a simple and profound meaning.

The boat grounded blindly at the very spot from which we had set off.

FROM THE STREET, I saw a child's hand press flat against the misted windowpane, and wipe it from top to bottom. Through the opening thus cleared a little close-cropped head showed itself, with somewhat pallid, melancholy features that struck me as familiar. I walked up to the building and read the sign above the front steps: "Grammar School." The school where Vera taught . . .

I had come here by chance after making long detours in search of the wooden church Otar and I had failed to find. The church stood at the entrance to the village of Nakhod, about six miles from Mirnoe on the far side of the lake. There were still stirrings of life there: three dozen houses, a dairy, a tractor repair shop (a building with a rusty corrugated iron roof), and this one-room schoolhouse.

I stole a glance in at the now-clean window. Ancient desks made of thick planks, with old-fashioned holes for inkwells, portraits of writers (Pushkin's flowing locks, Tolstoy's beard), and above the blackboard Lenin's piercing gaze. Several boys and girls were banging down their desk lids, sliding back onto the benches; clearly the first break had just finished. Vera got up from her chair, an exercise book in her hand.

I knocked discreetly and asked permission to come in, like a pupil arriving late. Her amazement was a little like the discomposure she had failed to conceal when I sat myself down in her *izba* at the far end of the bench, facing the window, her own lookout post. . . . But this time the discomposure was tinged with evident pleasure as well as irony, as she indicated a seat for me, murmuring: "Welcome, Comrade Inspector. . . ." I sat at the back, "the dunces' row," I thought, guessing from Vera's look that the same idea had struck her.

The children's coats were hung on the wall near a large brick stove with cracked plaster. The black stovepipe separated Chekhov's romantically myopic countenance from the Promethean gaze of the young Gorky. Prominent on top of a set of bookshelves was a terrestrial globe covered in dust and surrounded by a wire circle: the orbit of the moon, a silvered ball, long since wrenched from its path, which now lay upon a pile of old maps. A light haze arose from the wringing-wet garments, steaming up the windows. I pictured the waterlogged pathways covered in russet leaves that the children had followed to come here from their scattered villages in the depths of the forest. These misted windowpanes provoked thoughts of winter, and the fronds of hoarfrost that would soon be woven across them. "I'll be far away by then," I said to myself, and the idea of no longer being in these vast expanses of the North, no longer seeing this woman who was now walking from one desk to the next, suddenly seemed very strange to me.

There were eight pupils, all told. Judging from what they were doing, I quickly gauged the age differences: three boys and a girl were calculating the speed of two boats in pursuit of one another on the Volga–Don Canal. So, ten or eleven. Three younger pupils were taking turns to read out their written homework about a walk through the forest. The final one, sitting facing Vera's desk, was learning to write.

To begin with, I cocked an ear toward the terms in which the problem of the boats was presented, then confessed myself incapable of solving it, having forgotten everything about tricky arithmetical problems like this one. A ludicrous and tangible indication of the passage of time . . . And I started listening to the three stories of walks through the forest. The first told of the classic fear of wolves. The second, with poetic but dangerous imprecision, explained how to tell edible mushrooms from their poisonous doubles. . . . In a few polite words but without flattery Vera praised these fumbling descriptions.

The third account of a walk was the shortest. As it unfolded, there were no "carpets of beautiful golden leaves" nor "a wolf's great footprints," nor even a "deaf cap" (for "death cap") mushroom. . . . It was read out by the child I had caught sight of earlier through the cleared window. His face still had the same dreamy expression; one of the elbows of his old pullover was completely unraveled, the other, in a strange contrast, was carefully darned. His voice did not describe, it simply stated, insistently, as if to say: "All I can tell you is what I saw and what happened to me."

On the way to school the previous day, he said, he went into the forest to avoid a pathway the rains had transformed into a stream. He passed through a clearing he had never been in before. And there, tramping through the dead leaves, he disturbed a sleeping butterfly that flew away in the cold air. Where would it find shelter now when the snowstorms came?

The question was put in tones at once distraught and truculent, as if addressing a reproach to us all. The boy sat down, his eyes turned toward the window his hand had wiped clean, now cloudy once more. The other pupils, even the ones at the helm of their boats, looked up. There was a moment of silence. I saw that Vera was searching for words before concluding: "In the spring, Lyosha, you'll go back to that clearing and you'll see your butterfly. In fact, we'll all go together. . . . Yours is a very good story!" The boy shrugged his shoulders, as if to say: "But it's not a story. It's what I saw."

And then I recognized him. He was one of the sons of the man who had hanged himself by fastening the rope to the door of a shed at the beginning of September, the drunkard of whom I was planning to make a satirical portrait. I recalled the little crowd of his children, with staring eyes, no tears, and this boy's desperate flight across a piece of wasteland. . . . Now here he was, talking of a butterfly disturbed under a dead leaf, deprived of winter shelter.

Vera looked at her watch, announced another break. The children rushed outside; the youngest, the one who was learning to write, produced a bread-and-butter sandwich from his satchel. Lyosha removed his pullover and took it to Vera without a word. The shirt he was wearing underneath was a large man's shirt, taken in at the sides and with the sleeves shortened. He stayed in the classroom, leaning his back against the warm brick of the stove. Vera drew her chair up to the window, produced a scrap of cloth, a spool of thread, a needle. As she patched in silence, I looked at the books on the shelves, mainly textbooks, selected passages from classic authors, then, a completely ridiculous intrusion, *A Typology of Scandinavian Languages.* "Another piece of flotsam she's fished out of some wrecked library," I thought and went outside. Beneath a sloping roof, a stack of firewood, piled high, supplies for the winter. I took an ax and set about splitting thick ends of timber, stacking up the logs, which gave off a bitter aroma of fog. And once again the thought that this timber would be burning in the big stove in the classroom long after I had departed, the very idea of the fire I would never see, struck me as bizarre.

We returned home together on foot, walking slowly around the lake. Unfamiliar at first, the track quickly joined the one I had always taken, leading from the old landing stage, by way of the crossroads and the signpost with the mailbox, to the willow groves where I had surprised the woman hauling in her fishing net. . . . In the middle of the lake, the clear curves of the church stood out in the mist-laden air on the ochreous hump of the island.

"One should have no illusions," Vera said, when I talked to her about her pupils. "The only possible future for them is to go away. We're not even living in the past here. We're in the pluperfect. These children will go off to towns where their best hope will be work on a construction site, up to their ears in mud, a young workers' barracks, alcohol, violence. But, you know, I sometimes tell myself that something of these forests will stay with them all the same. And our lessons. A butterfly awakened just before winter. If young Lyosha thought about that, he'll surely hold on to some trace of it. Despite his drunken father's death, despite the filth of the towns he'll soon be immersed in. Despite everything. It's not much, of course. And yet, I'm sure such things can save people. Often just a little thing can be enough to keep one from going under."

As we passed close by the spot she used to fish from, on the shoreline covered by the bare willow groves, I sensed that the memory of our first encounter still lingered within her, for she lost no time in breaking the silence, talking with some embarrassment, looking away and pointing to the island. "One of the Vikings' routes to the south passed this spot. They would see that island just the same as it is now, minus the church and graveyard. In their language they called it *holm*, an island. Whereas in Russian *holm* means a hill. It's a question for the specialist. Why this shift in meaning?"

Taken aback, I mumbled: "Oh, some kind of etymological perversity, I guess. . . . Maybe the Russians drank more than the Scandinavians. . . . Though they do say the

Finns can run rings round us in that department.... Wait a minute ... So with us a Viking island turns into a hill? All right. I give up. Tell me about these Norsemen and their *holm*."

"Well, to begin with, we're talking about Swedes and Norwegians, not Finns. When they came here on their raids, they needed a considerable draw for their heavy dragon ships. So they preferred to come in the spring, during the high tides. Thanks to these, even the villages generally far away from the shore came within their reach. They saw an island and yelled, 'Holm!' The natives remembered the word and used it to refer to what this 'island' became when the waters retreated. Simply a hill in the middle of the fields, once again laid bare. I'm sorry if all that sounds pedantic. When I was young, I embarked on a thesis about all this etymological humbug. But fortunately I never completed the course—"

"A thesis? You mean a doctoral thesis?" My astonishment was such that I slowed my pace, almost to a standstill. This obscure schoolteacher, this Vera, forgotten by everyone in this remote neck of the woods ... A doctorate in linguistic studies! It seemed like a joke.

"So where did you study?" There was ill-concealed skepticism in my voice and also a degree of irritation: here in this northern wilderness, with my university diploma, I believed I was erudition incarnate. Now, mortified, I realized that my own self-esteem had been dented by this upheaval in the intellectual hierarchy.

"In Leningrad, at the university. I had Ivanitsky as my thesis supervisor. You probably didn't know him. He died at the end of the sixties. He was very upset with me for throwing in the towel just before it came to defending my thesis. . . ."

I listened to her, unable to tune out the conflicting images: a recluse, an inconsolable fiancée-widow, a hermit dedicated to the cult of the dead, and this young research student in the Leningrad of the sixties with all that post-Stalin ferment. I quickly added five years of university studies to three years on the thesis, that is to say at least eight long years spent far from the forests of Mirnoe. A whole lifetime! So I had been completely mistaken about the sense of her life here. . . .

I followed her automatically. Without noticing that we had reached the village, I walked straight past the *izba* where I lodged and into her house, as if this were what always happened, as if we were a couple.

Once inside the main room, I came to my senses and studied the interior, which now gave evidence of a totally different way of life: books on linguistics, perfectly normal reading for her, of course, reproductions hung on the walls, some of whose subjects needed to be viewed as tongue-in-cheek humor, as in the case of a landscape captioned: "On the pack ice: family of polar bears." A neatness owing more to intellectual discipline than the whims of an old maid. And that spot at the end of the bench, her lookout post, which she had readily abandoned to go to Leningrad or elsewhere. A different woman . . .

I remained standing as I spoke, still feeling I had lost my bearings in this transformed space.

"But why did you come back?" My urgency in asking her gave away the real question: Why, after so many years spent in Leningrad, come and bury yourself here among the drunkards and the bears?

She must have been aware of the implication, but replied without any hint of solemnity, as she continued making the tea: "I had a funny feeling during all those years in Leningrad. I was more or less content with what I was doing there, quite involved in their life—you'll note I said, 'their life,'" she smiled. "And yet very divided. As if this interlude at the university was a way of proving to other people that I belonged elsewhere. You see, for me there was something very artificial about those years of the thaw. Something hypocritical. They pilloried Stalin but sanctified Lenin more than ever. It was a fairly understandable sleight of hand. After the collapse of one cult, people were clinging to the last remaining idols. I remember very fashionable poets appearing in stadiums before tens of thousands of people. One of them declaimed: 'Take Lenin's picture off our banknotes. For he is beyond price!' It was inspiring, new, intoxicating. And false. Most of the people who applauded those lines knew the first concentration camps had been built on Lenin's orders. And as for barbed wire, by the way, there was never any shortage of that in these parts, around Mirnoe. But the poets preferred to lie. That was why they were showered with honors and dachas in the Crimea. . . ."

She poured tea for us, offered me a chair, sat down at the far end of the bench. . . . I listened to her with the strange sensation of hearing not the story of the democratic hopes of the sixties but that of the following decade, of the seventies, of our dissident youth: poems, rallies, alcohol, and freedom.

No doubt her remarks about the privileges accorded to the poets struck her as too caustic, for she smiled and added: "It was probably mainly my fault if I didn't manage to be at ease at that time. I argued, read carbon copies of dissident texts, did my research on the typology of Old Swedish and Russian. But I wasn't living."

She fell silent, her gaze lost in the gray light of the dusk outside the window. I thought I could detect in her eyes the reflection of the fields with their dead vegetation, the crossroads, the dark terracing of the forest.

"Besides, the way it all happened was much simpler

than that. I came back to Mirnoe to . . . bury my mother. I planned to stay for nine days, as tradition seems to demand. Then for forty. And one thing led to another. . . . To crown it all, there were several old women here already, hardly more robust than my mother had been. No, there were no regrets. No conflict. I simply realized my place was here. Or, at least, I didn't even think about it. I started living again."

She stood up to put the kettle back on the fire. I turned my head, glanced quickly out the window: with growing, dreamlike clarity, the shadowy figure of a man on foot detached itself from the forest.

Vera returned, set down some toast, refilled our cups. What she said now sounded mainly like an inner rumination, a rehearsal of old arguments, perfectly convincing to her, only spoken out loud because I was there. "I also realized that up here in Mirnoe all those debates we had in Leningrad, whether anti-Soviet or pro-Soviet, meant nothing. Coming here, I found half a dozen very old women who'd lost their families in the war and were going to die. As simple as that. Human beings getting ready to die alone, not complaining, not seeking someone to blame. Before I got to know them, I had never thought about God, truly, profoundly. . . ."

She broke off, noticing my gaze sidling along the bookshelf (in fact, I was suddenly finding it hard to look her in the eye). She smiled, indicating the row of volumes with a little jerk of her chin. "At any rate, I was already too old for the university. I looked like a hearty kolkhoznik among all those young students in miniskirts."

The light faded, Vera reached for the switch, then changed her mind, struck a match. The flame of a candle placed on the windowsill glowed, plunging the fields and pathways outside the glass into darkness. She sat down in her usual spot, we listened to the silence punctuated by the wind, and all at once a slight creak, the sigh of an old beam, a door frame feeling its age.

Her eyes remained calm, but her eyelashes fluttered rapidly. As if I were no longer there, she murmured: "Besides, how can I leave? I'm still waiting for him."

DURING THAT TEN-MILE EXPEDITION on an icy, luminous October day, I became quite certain I was sharing the reality of Vera's life. Once more we followed the track she used to take to go to her school. The willow plantations beside the lake, the crossroads with the mailbox, the old landing stage . . . There, a footpath veered off northward into the depths of the forest.

Some days earlier, one of her pupils had told her about a hamlet lost amid the undergrowth where only one inhabitant remained, a deaf, almost blind old woman, according to him, whose name he had not been able to discover, not even her Christian name. Vera had gone to see the head of the neighboring kolkhoz, hoping to obtain a truck. She had been told that for these overgrown paths a tank was what she really needed. . . . So that Saturday she knocked on my door and we set off, dragging behind us a comic vehicle perched on odd bicycle wheels: a little cart that had belonged to a soldier from Mirnoe, who had returned legless from the front and died shortly after the war.

The cold eased our journey through the forest, where the muddy tracks were frozen solid, even making it possible to walk across peat bogs. From time to time we stopped to catch our breath, and also to pick a handful of cranberries, for all the world like tiny scoops of sorbet that melted slowly in the mouth, sharp and icy.

It was possibly the first time since we met that our actions, words, and silences came so naturally. I felt as if there were nothing more for me to guess at, nothing more to understand. To me her life had the clarity of these stained-glass windows of sky inlaid between the dark crowns of the fir trees.

"Self-denial, altruism"; subconsciously, this woman's character still provoked phrases in my mind that were attempts to define it. But they all failed in the face of the impulsive simplicity with which Vera acted. This led me to the conclusion that good (Good!) is a complex thing and conducive to pompous language as soon as one makes a moral issue of it, a debating topic. But it becomes humble and clear from the first real step in its direction:

this walk through the forest, this prosaically muscular effort that dispersed the edifying fantasies of the good conscience. Besides, what looked to others like a good deed was for Vera nothing more than a habit of long standing. "It wouldn't be a bad idea if we picked a few mushrooms on the way back," she said, during a halt. "I could cook them for the old woman tomorrow."

The hamlet, hemmed in by the increasingly invasive forest, suddenly opened up before us and seemed uninhabited. Trees grew in the middle of the street, and some of the roofs had collapsed, revealing the spindly framework of beams beneath the layers of thatch. We went into twelve houses in turn, trying to spot the likeliest signs of human habitation. Ragged washing on a line in a yard? We went in: the floor was rotten, gave way easily underfoot. . . . No, well, how about this *izba*? On the wooden front steps, a rusty bicycle, balanced upside down on its seat and handlebars, looked as if it were waiting for the repairman to appear in the doorway, tools in hand. The house was empty; at the windows with their broken panes dried plant stems quivered in the draft. . . .

There was one house whose door we almost failed to try. The roof beams pointed skyward like the broken ribs of a carcass. The windows had lost their carved-wood frames. The front steps were almost hidden by dense undergrowth. We were about to go on our way. . . . Suddenly, this voice. It came from a very low bench that ran the length of the wall and was hidden by the bushes. An old woman sat there, with half closed eyes, a cat curled up on her lap, to which she was reciting a litany of soothing words. She saw us, stood up, depositing the cat on the bench, and, in ringing tones, astonishingly forceful for her frail body, invited us to come in. There, an even greater surprise awaited us.

The sky was visible through the partly collapsed roof, and this space open to the four winds had been rearranged in a way one would never have dreamed of: another, much smaller house had been built in the middle of the room, a miniature *izba*, fashioned out of the planks from some shed or fence. A real roof, a low, narrow door, doubtless salvaged from a barn, a window. The ruin that surrounded it already belonged to the outside world, its stormy weather, its wild nights. Nature held sway there. But the new edifice offered a replica, in condensed form, of the lost comforts. Bent double, we went in and discovered the austerity of a primitive life and astonishing neatness. A kind of vital minimum, I noted in my mind, the final frontier between human existence and the cosmos. A very small bed, a table, a stool, two plates, a cup, and on the wall, the dark rectangle of an icon, surrounded by several yellowed letters.

Especially clever was the way this dwelling had been annexed onto the brickwork of the great stove that occupied half of the ruined house. As she showed us around her doll's house, the old woman explained that in winter she would go out into the main room invaded by snow, light the fire in the stove, then take refuge in her tiny *izba*. . . . Contrary to what we had been told about her, she was not deaf, just a little hard of hearing, but her sight was going, her vision was shrinking, just as the size of her world-within-a-world was growing smaller.

At one moment during the visit, Vera signaled to me discreetly that she wanted to be left alone with the old woman.

I walked over to the pond, at the center of which the outline of a sunken boat could just be made out. In the house next door, I came upon a pile of school textbooks, a notebook filled with grammar exercises. I was struck by a sentence, copied out to illustrate some rule of syntax that must be observed: "The defenders of Leningrad obeyed Stalin's order to resist to the last drop of their blood." No, not syntax. It was more the gradation of sounds. I had need of these ironic little insights in order to bear the weight of time stagnating in a thick pool of absurdity in every one of these houses, in the empty street.

"Soon Mirnoe will look exactly like this," I thought,

making my way back to the old survivor's *izba*. "Just as empty of people. More fossilized than the rules of grammar."

The two women had already reemerged and were bustling around the little cart with bicycle wheels. I could readily imagine the course their private negotiations had followed. At first, the old woman's refusal to leave, a refusal made for form's sake but necessary to justify her long years of solitude, to avoid acknowledging that she had been abandoned. Next, Vera making her case, weighing every word, for the hermit must not be robbed of her only remaining pride, that of being capable of dying alone. . . . Then, from one phrase to the next, an imperceptible rapprochement, the convergence of their life histories as women, empathy and finally the admissions each made, this one above all: the fear of dying alone.

I went over to them, offered my help. I saw they both had slightly reddened eyes. I reflected on my ironic reaction just now when reading that sentence about Stalin ordering the defense of Leningrad. Such had been the sarcastic tone prevalent in our dissident intellectual circle. A humor that provided real mental comfort, for it placed us above the fray. Now, observing these two women who had just shed a few tears as they reached their decision, I sensed that our irony was in collision with something that went beyond it. "Rustic sentimentality," would have been our sneering comment at the Wigwam. *"Les misérables,* Soviet-style . . ." Such mockery would have been wide of the mark, I now knew. What was essential was these women's hands loading the totality of a human being's material existence onto the little cart.

The totality! The notion staggered me. Everything the old woman needed was there, on the three short planks of our cart. She went into the *izba,* came back with the icon wrapped in a piece of cotton fabric.

"Katerina Ivanovna's coming with us," said Vera, as if referring to a brief visit or an excursion. "But she doesn't want to ride in our taxi. She prefers to walk. We'll see. . . ."

She drew me a little ahead to let the old woman say her farewells to the house. Katerina went up to the front steps, crossed herself, bowing very low, crossed herself again, came to join us. Her cat followed her at a distance.

As we entered the forest, I thought about the first night that village was going to spend without a living soul. Katerina's *izba*-within-an-*izba,* the bench where in summer she used to await the appearance of a favorite star, that notebook with the grammar exercise from Stalin's time. "When a certain degree of depletion is reached," I thought, "life ceases to be about things. Then, and only then, may be the moment when the need to recount it in a book becomes overwhelming. . . ."

About two o'clock in the afternoon, the footpaths began to thaw. In some places I had to carry Katerina, striding over chasms in the mud. Her body had the ethereal lightness of old clothes.

By evening, the new arrival was completely settled in. Above the *izba* Vera had chosen for her a bluish wisp of smoke hung in the air, with the scent of birch logs burning in the stove. The line of the roof and the dark crenellations of the forest stood out against the purple sky with the sharpness of a silverpoint drawing, then, blurred by a transparent puff of smoke, they began to sway gently. As did that star in the north, which was growing similarly restless and coming closer.

I saw Vera slowly crossing the street, her arms weighed down with full pails. She stopped for a moment, setting her load down on the ground, remained motionless, her gaze directed toward the broad expanse of the lake that was still light.

Goodness, altruism, sharing . . . All this struck me now as much too cerebral, too bookish. Our day had had no other objective than the beauty of this haze of smoke with its scent of burning birch bark, the lively dancing of the star, the silence of this woman in the middle of the road, her silhouette etched against the opal of the lake.

"When a certain degree of depletion is reached," I recalled, "reality ceases to be about things and becomes the word. When a certain degree of suffering is reached, the pain allows us to perceive fully the immediate beauty of each moment. . . ."

The absence of sound was such that at a distance, I heard a faint sigh. Vera lifted up her pails once more, made her way toward Katerina's house. It occurred to me that the old woman was experiencing all that happened to her now—the wood fire scent, the lake outside the window of her new house—as the start of an afterlife, given that she had long since accepted the idea of dying alone, given that for other people dead was what she already was.

In Leningrad, at the Wigwam, we were forever making clear-cut distinctions between good and evil in the world. I knew the evil that had laid waste to these villages in the North was boundless. And yet never had the world appeared so beautiful to me as that night, seen through the eyes of a tired old woman. Beautiful and worthy of being protected by words against the swift erasure of our deeds.

I spent several days in the solemn, serene conviction that I had achieved full insight into the mystery of Vera's life.

And then one Saturday evening, a week after our expedition, I saw her setting off toward the crossroads where, at the end of the day, one could wait for a truck going to the district capital. She was not wearing her old cavalry greatcoat but a beige raincoat of an elegant cut, which I was seeing for the first time. She had put up her hair into a full chignon on the nape of her neck. She was walking briskly and looked very much like a woman on her way to meet a man—which I found quite incredible.

As I DRESSED HURRIEDLY, ran out into the street, cut through the undergrowth, and headed for the crossroads, the echo of one of Otar's mocking remarks rang in my ears: "You're an artist. You need beauty and tenderness. . . ."

Nothing wounds more bitterly than conventional sexuality in a woman one has idealized. The existence I had dreamed up for Vera was a beautiful lie. The truth lay hidden in this woman's body, a woman who, very healthily, once a week (or more often?) slept with a man, her lover (a married man? a widower?), came back to Mirnoe, went on looking after the old women . . .

I ran, stumbling over roots hidden under leaves, then stopped, out of breath, one hand leaning against a tree trunk. It was as if the mist from my breath in the frozen air endowed the scenes I imagined with a physical authenticity. A house, a door opening in a fence, a kiss, the warmth of a room, a dinner with rich country cooking, drinks, a very high double bed beneath an ancient clock, the woman's body, with thighs parted wide, moans of pleasure . . . The devastating and wholly natural obviousness of this coupling, its complete human legitimacy. And the utter impossibility of conceiving of it, given that only yesterday evening one could still hallucinate the appearance of a soldier returning home at this very crossroads.

I reached the meeting of the ways at the moment when the two rear lights of a truck that had just passed were fading into the dusk. My quarry must have boarded it. She would climb down, knock at a gate, kiss the man who opened it. There would be the dinner, the high double bed, the body offered with mature, generous, feminine savoir faire . . .

So this love affair, long ago embedded in her daily routine, had always coexisted comfortably with everything else: retrieving elderly survivors, the lake's nocturnal beauty . . .

And even her wait for the soldier! For she knew very well he would never come back. On the one hand, the peace she brought to lonely old women, her own solitude, the radiance of those autumn moments we had lived through together on the island. And on the other . . .

this pleasure taken in the depths of a double bed. Only in my fantasies did such a mixture seem impossible. But life, easygoing life, caring little for elegance, is nothing more than a constant mixture of genres.

Another truck might come in five minutes, or in five hours. In all likelihood, I would have to beat a retreat, and in any case, I thought, with a brief dawning of lucidity, how would I find her in the town? And above all, why should I find her? A perfectly grotesque scene enacted itself inside my head: I am in front of a great wooden gate, barring the way to a woman, this woman who has come to make love with a man: I thrust her back, reminding her indignantly that the soldier may return. . . .

A beam of light drew me out of this delirium. A motorcycle pulled up. I recognized the deputy director of the cultural center. The motorcycle was the key feature of the role he affected: dark and brooding, hard but romantic, misunderstood by his time. His powerful machine would have needed good asphalt roads for the performance to carry conviction, but we began jolting painfully along, bouncing from one rut to the next, sometimes raising our legs to protect them from spurts of mud. Around a corner, red reflectors gleamed at us; the deputy director let fly an oath. We were now compelled to crawl along for mile after mile amid the noise and stink of the truck.

I asked to get down at the edge of the town, where the truck came to a halt. Before he drove off, the biker called out through the noise of his backfiring machine: "Come to my house this evening! It's a farewell party for Otar. . . ." And in an abrupt, aggressive maneuver, he overtook the truck. Vera was already walking away down a street lit by a pallid neon tube attached to the façade of a store.

It was not hard for me to follow her in the darkness. She turned off into a wider street (Marx Avenue, I noted distractedly), cut through a square, seemed to linger in front of a store window (the town's only department store), quickened her pace. A minute later, we found ourselves on the platform at the railroad station, separated by an impatient and visibly excited crowd. Everyone was waiting for the Moscow train to pass through, the most important daily event in the life of the town.

She hung back, close to a pile of old railroad ties at one end of the platform. From time to time, edged out by people who moved in close to her, she moved away furtively and was then obliged to slip into the crowd, to sidle into a fresh hiding place without being recognized. Amid this gathering, all in their Sunday best, the two of us were both hunter and hunted, for as she drew near, I would back away, ready to cut and run, making myself scarce like a thief taking fright. And even though I might lose sight of her for several seconds, I felt I could sense her presence, like the warm pulsing of a vein, in among all these overcoats covered in frozen mist.

When in the distance the locomotive's headlamp pierced the fog, the crowd stirred, pressed closer to the tracks, and to my alarm, I saw that Vera was only a couple of steps away from me, her eyes following the coaches as they streamed past. I moved away, clambered over the first of the suitcases that were being set down on the ground, deafened by noisy hugs and kisses, jostled by coalescing families. I looked back but did not see her again. Slowly the platform emptied; the only ones left now were those who had been let down and the most daring of the smokers, poised to leap back on board the train as soon as the whistle blew. She was no longer there. "A man with a slight nick on his chin from shaving in a swaying railroad car, pungent eau de cologne, a dinner over which he'll recount the latest news from the capital, a high double bed, their sleep together. . . ."

As I left the station, I told myself that sleeping in a man's arms might well be the most natural, even the most honorable, solution for Vera, a way of life she was deprived of when others' eyes were focused on her, banal, to be sure, but one to which she had truly earned the right. I almost convinced myself. Then suddenly I realized I was filled with contempt both for such a way of life and for such a woman.

The party was already in full swing at the deputy director's. The room, blue with tobacco smoke, was very unevenly lit by candles. Voices were getting louder, men laughing, women shrieking, from which it was easy to deduce their levels of intoxication. I sat down beside one of the women guests and, beneath her garish makeup, recognized the features of the history teacher. I was given wine. (Georgian wine, I noted. Otar must have cleared out his cellar.) Someone yelled out a toast in welcome. I drank hastily, eager to catch up with them in their boisterous merriment. They were already chorusing yet another toast in celebration of Otar's freedom regained.

I did not notice the moment when our bickering and chaotic conversation touched on Mirnoe. Had I provoked this myself? Unlikely. I was only half listening and did not realize they were talking about Vera until the history teacher exclaimed: "Oh, yes. A hermit, a nun. You could have fooled me! She fucks left, right, and center. What do you mean: 'Who with?' With the stationmaster, for heaven's sake. And I'll tell you another thing. . . ." Her voice was drowned by other voices and other remarks.

The pain of what I had just heard sobered me instantly. I found myself sitting on the ground on a rolled-up sheepskin, my arm tightly clasping the woman as she continued yelling, my right hand kneading her breast, her skintight sweater sticky under the armpit.

So life was nothing more than this carnal stickiness, men's and women's desire, pawing one another, possessing one another, moving on. "First they're on fire. After, they tire . . ." Everything else was lies told by poets. Slipping out of her skirt, the history teacher leaned forward and, with rounded lips, as if for a caricature of a kiss, blew out a candle. In the dim light other bodies were tightening their knots of arms, necks, and legs. I heard Otar's sad laugh. The art teacher angrily explaining that for children to be taught painting properly, they needed to begin with Malevich's *Black Square on a White Field.* She had not found a man to make love with that evening. Someone made a joke about the whole of Russia being electrified, and I realized that the candles were not there to create an atmosphere but were needed because of a power failure. Their light was sufficient for me to make out the pattern on the fabric of the undergarments my partner was in the process of discarding: something green and flowery. And as always in such hasty couplings, only half desired by the participants, a glimmer of wry pity crept in, for this alien body, so touching in its zeal to simulate love. All at once indifference took over, then the simple desire to crush those warm, bare breasts . . .

The shout that went up was excessive in relation to the extent of the catastrophe, as we quickly realized. A candle had fallen off a windowsill and rolled under a curtain; the blaze was spectacular. The hysterical yell of "Fire!" came in response to this first impression of an inferno. Panic contributed to it. Orders issued and countermanded, half-naked bodies rushing this way and that, smoke. But already the guilty curtain lay upon the ground, furiously trampled on by several pairs of feet. Finally, sighs of relief all around, a moment of stasis after extreme frenzy, then astonishment: the electricity had come back on again!

We stood there, blinking, staring at one another upon this amorous battlefield, over which filaments of soot floated. Smeared makeup, pale masculine chests, but one thing, above all!

Laughter suddenly erupted, swelled, and at its peak reached the pitch that brings it close to tears: the history teacher, the librarian, and the nurse were all wearing completely identical underwear, the only type available in the only department store in the district capital, as displayed by the unique female mannequin in the shop window. The art teacher was laughing more than the rest. She still had her clothes on, having been unable to find a partner, and was exacting her revenge for an unrewarding evening. And the cassette player, coming back to life, struck up in hoarse, mellow tones: ". . . When the birdlings wake and cry, I love you . . ."

The laughter continued, in little bursts, increasingly

forced. We were trying to postpone the ending of this merriment, aware sadness was imminent. A rude awakening in a cold house in a room that smelled of canned fish, stale bodies, and the bitter reek of a fire nipped in the bud. The day was about to dawn. Then someone noticed Otar's absence; that saved the situation. There was a flood of jokes about the sexual appetites of Georgians. Real men who refuse to be disturbed in the act, even by a house catching fire! A bottle was uncorked, the lights were turned off, people wandered about indecisively in the hope that the night, and their dampened desires, might gain a new lease on life.

I saw Otar when I went out. Contrary to our malicious gossip, he was perched outside on the handrail to the front steps, smoking. The broad brim of his fedora was dripping with rain. "Shall we go?" he said, as if we had planned to leave together. "The only thing is, I don't have my truck anymore. I gave it back." He gave a wry smile and added: "In exchange for my freedom."

At this moment the door opened, and the master of the house presented me with a long cape of tent canvas and two bottles of liquor. I was still enjoying some privileges thanks to my standing as a Leningrad intellectual.

In two hours' time, Otar was due to catch the train for Moscow, the one I had waited for the previous evening. He went with me to the edge of the town, to the highway where, early in the morning, one could get a ride on one of the vast trucks carrying pine tree trunks. When we heard the throbbing of the vehicle, he quickly took a brown paper envelope out of his bag, thrust it into my hands, and growled, at once embarrassed and commanding: "There. Put that in the mailbox. You know the one. At the crossroads. It's for her. . . ." Then he clapped me heavily on the shoulder, scratched my cheek with his beard, and went to place himself in the roadway to stop the truck.

From time to time, chatting with the driver in the smoke-filled cab, I fingered the rough thickness of the envelope beneath the canvas of my cape.

The rectangle slid into the box, which reverberated with an empty sound. So many hopes linked to this hollow piece of ironmongery! Ah, those hopes . . . It all came back to me now: the man getting off the Moscow train yesterday and his eau de cologne, a dinner, a high bed, a woman moaning with pleasure. So Otar was just as gullible as me. "An artist who needs beauty and tenderness . . ."

The rain abated; I turned back the hood of my cape and inhaled as if emerging into the open air. The morning resembled a bleak, icy dusk, the clay, churned up by tracked vehicles, was reminiscent of a road in wartime. I rounded the corner of the forest, turned off onto the track leading to Mirnoe. The village soon came into view through the gray mist and looked to me more barren than the deserted villages I had been visiting during the past two months of my wanderings.

And the most uninhabited house of all was this one, this *izba* with pretty lace curtains at the windows. The woman who lived there must at that very moment be asleep in the arms of a man, somewhere in the town. A double bed warmed by their bodies heavy with love, the masculine eau de cologne mingling with the bitter, sugary tang of Red Moscow perfume . . .

When I was twenty yards away from the front steps, the door opened. I saw Vera's silhouette, watched her recoil abruptly, disappear. An empty pail fell down the steps, rolled onto the ground with a metallic clatter. I drew closer, the door was shut, and the house again looked abandoned. I hesitated to knock, picked up the pail, set it back on the steps. After several seconds of pacing up and down beneath the windows, I continued on my way without having really understood what had just happened.

In my head, clouded with alcohol and the futile words uttered during our sleepless night, I put two and two together: if she had come home so early in the morning, Vera could not have spent that night with a lover, unless she had returned in the dark, by roads barely fit for motor vehicles even in broad daylight. Or else it was a brief coupling, that simulation of love I had almost engaged in with the history teacher. "Life is nothing more than the sticky warmth of a woman's armpit," I recalled, with nausea. Suddenly an impulsive, wild joy, too wild for the quite simple conclusion that had provoked it: the woman who had just let that pail drop had met no one and had come home all alone, as she always did.

I looked around me. The chill pewter of the lake, the dark timbers of the facade of the former administrative center . . . And this mirror broken in half, abandoned beside the worm-eaten front steps. I stopped, glanced into its murky surface, streaked with raindrops. And, as Vera had done, I recoiled momentarily. . . .

A soldier, clad in a long cape, dark with rain, his boots heavy with mud from the pathways, had his calm, grave stare fixed upon me.

THREE

As she talked, she seemed both focused and distracted. Underneath the table, which, in anticipation of her visit, I had covered with a square of cloth, I saw she had kicked off her shoes. Red slippers of a type that must have been in fashion a dozen years before lay on their sides in the manner of a woman's shoes carelessly discarded below a bed of love. Shoes possibly too tight for her now. Their heels were coated with earth, from the mass of clay on the hundred yards that lay between our two *izbas.* As she talked, her eyes were mesmerized by the dazzle of a candle flame reflected in a glass. Candles, the husky sweetness of a jazz singer . . . It was my attempt to create a mood.

"Why lie? I sometimes really dread it. Him coming back . . . My life's behind me now. . . . But even in the early days, I was afraid of his return. . . . When I saw you wearing that military cape yesterday, it gave me the fright of my life. What to say first, what to do first . . . I've spent thirty years rehearsing it all, and suddenly I was at a complete loss."

I let her talk, as one does with a person under hypnosis, trying not to interrupt as they unburden themselves. My curiosity was mingled with a powerful sense that we were getting close to the truth. More than her words, it was her body, the relaxed posture of her body, that revealed the ultimate truth about her life. A woman like her, an impassive idol, unyielding in the face of the weather, indifferent to fate, could also be this: a woman mellowed by two glasses of sweet liqueur, her cheeks rosy like a young girl's, artless confidences tinged with the sentimentality of a provincial old maid, the evident delight taken in a "candlelit supper," a "sophisticated" evening, with a background of languid mood music, and the lazy strains of: "When the dawn flames in the sky, I love you. . . ."

Yes, life, the real thing, that perpetual mixture of genres.

Proud of this wisdom, new found for me, I was playing the hypnotist, pouring the wine, changing the tapes, asking questions in a scarcely audible murmur so that the sleeper should not awaken.

"The other day I saw you going off in the evening, where did you go?"

"Yesterday, no, the day before yesterday, I went to the station . . . I waited for the Moscow train . . . I find myself doing it from time to time. The dream's nearly always the same. It's night, the platform, he's getting off the train, coming toward me . . . This time it was, if anything, more real than ever. I was certain he'd come. I went there. I waited. None of it makes any sense, I know. But if I hadn't gone, a link would have been broken . . . And there'd be no point in waiting anymore. . . ."

Her eyelids batted slowly; she looked up at me with a fond, dreamy gaze that did not see me, would only see me when the shadows flitting across it had passed. I sensed that during this blindness I could have taken any liberty. I could have seized her hand. I was already touching this hand; my fingers moved lightly along her forearm. We were sitting side by side, and the sensation of having this woman in my possession was infinitely powerful and infinitely touching. Almost in a whisper I asked: "And when you saw no one was there, did you come straight home?"

I felt I had found the rhythm and the timbre that did not risk arousing her from her waking sleep. My hand gently enfolded her shoulder; the movement, if she had abruptly come to herself, could still have been taken for one of friendly familiarity occasioned by the festive evening and the wine.

"Yes, I came home. . . . But maybe for the first time in my life, I wanted to . . . To forget myself. To forget everything. To let my hair down like a teenager. You know, let it all hang out. Like now, with this kind of silly music and the wine . . ."

Her shoulder was gently pressing into my chest, and when she spoke, the physical vibrations from the sound of her voice reverberated within me. Nothing came between our bodies now, apart from her white silk blouse, chaste and old-fashioned in style, and the shadows slowly slipping away from her gaze. My arm eased gently along her shoulder, slid around her waist. Her hair smelled of birch leaves soaked in hot water. . . .

For several seconds we contrived by tacit agreement not to notice the noise. To take it for the insistent tapping of a branch of the sorb apple tree against the windowpane, stirred by the breeze from the White Sea. But there was no wind that night. We moved apart, looked toward the window. Half of a face, stained yellow by the candlelight, was observing us from outside. A little fist, tightly clenched, vibrated against the pane. In the rapid look that passed between us could be sensed our alarm and, above all, the absurdity of this alarm, this dread of a ghost. Vera adjusted her blouse; I went to the door while she felt for her shoes under the table. On the front steps stood Maria, a little bent old woman who lived in the *izba* next door to the bathhouse.

"Katerina's sick. Very sick. You need to go see her. . . ."

She said it without looking at me, as if Vera were the only person in the room. Rustic good manners, I thought, backing toward the wall. Accompanied by the old woman, Vera went out, slipping on her raincoat in the street, as country doctors do when awakened in the middle of the night. While putting away the remains of our supper, I told myself with mocking resentment that this intervention by fate (no, Fate!) would doubtless give rise to a thousand interpretations and reflections during Vera's long nocturnal soliloquies that winter. And I had a fierce desire to challenge this much-vaunted fate, to outmaneuver the guardian angel who had appeared in the guise of a shriveled little old woman.

I DID SO THE NEXT DAY by inviting Vera to visit me again, just to show her somewhat playfully that we could easily thwart fortune's dirty tricks and that time was still on our side. I felt myself all the more within my rights in doing so, since at noon I had seen the local doctor emerging from Katerina's house. With a sigh of irritation directed at Vera, who was just behind him, he said: "Well, at her age, you know . . ." What his tone implied was: There you go, gathering up all these ancient ruins with one foot in the grave and I'm supposed to bruise my backside over thirty miles of potholes. . . . I remembered that the priest who came to visit Anna, when she was dying, had displayed exactly the same sullen face.

For a moment, I was afraid Vera might refuse to

come. She readily accepted and came bearing a bottle of wine and a dish of salted mushrooms: "You remember. We picked them when we went to fetch Katerina."

Strangely enough, it was her directness that held me back. Everything began to happen as it had the night before, but this time I knew that at any minute now this woman with her mature, statuesque body would be naked in my arms. Yet the body was a minor consideration. The woman naked in my arms would be the woman who for thirty years now . . . It seemed absolutely inconceivable. My behavior became self-conscious. I roared with laughter while feeling my features frozen. . . . Now ribbing her with absurd familiarity, now inhibited, almost tongue-tied.

Very quickly, she became the one leading the conversation, serving us, transforming my clumsy advances into harmless little blunders. Over dessert, just after salvaging one of these inept maneuvers by making a joke of it (when my hand settled on her forearm, it instantly seemed more out of place than a hammer would have been among our teacups), she began to talk about Alexandra Kollontai.

"Each generation has its own way of making passes. When I was in Leningrad in the sixties, the men who accosted you, and were anxious to cut to the chase, could only talk of one thing: Kollontai's 'glass of water theory.' Amid the ferment of the revolution, Alexandra Kollontai, a great beauty and a great friend of Lenin, came up with this proposition: satisfying your carnal instinct is as straightforward as drinking a glass of water. It seemed such a vital issue that during the early years following 1917, they were quite seriously planning to erect cabins in the streets of Moscow where the citizens could satisfy their physical desire. The best way of making passes is not to make a pass at all. To get straight to the point. You meet in the street. You find the nearest cabin. You drink your 'glass of water.' You go your separate ways. One in the eye for bourgeois propriety. But Lenin quickly condemned this theory as the product of left-wing deviation. And with a telling argument the young would do well to heed. 'However thirsty you are,' he said, 'you're still not going to drink from a murky pond. . . .' Have a little discernment, for goodness sake! So when in the sixties, a young man invited me to share that glass of water with him under the halo of Alexandra's moral authority, I had a ready-made and very Leninist reply: 'Take a look, young man. This aged crone you see in front of you. Doesn't she remind you of a stagnant pond?' It worked pretty well. . . ."

She got up, made some more tea, turned over the tape that had just stopped. Sitting there stiffly, emptied of all my prepared speeches, I was thinking of the seventies generation, our own way of making passes. It was a good deal less daring than the revolutionary glass of water. Tremulous mood music, candles, a bottle of imported liquor, and to crown it all, an American journalist as tangible proof of our commitment to dissidence. Apart from that, nothing had changed, bodies seeking to couple, that was all. Which was what Vera had wanted to make me realize by talking about Alexandra Kollontai.

"And what became of her later?"

I was genuinely curious to know, even though my question sounded like an attempt to extricate myself from my embarrassment.

Vera thought for a moment, like someone recalling an episode from her own life. She sat down and seemed less on her guard than at the outset, slightly sleepy, her gaze, as on the previous evening, entranced by the gleam of a candle.

"Later . . . later she married. Well, it was a very open marriage, to a man fifteen years her junior, a dashing red commissar, a Cossack who had the gall to countermand orders from Lenin himself. She had all kinds of adventures, military and amorous. She had affairs with women, too, it seems. And then she grew old, and her husband fell in love with another woman. And it wasn't like a glass of water. It was the real thing this time. She suffered agonies of jealousy. After fighting so hard against that bourgeois prejudice. And then, in a letter, she admitted that such simple and grievous things existed as a woman's age, exclusive attachment to one person, the unbearable pain of losing that person, faithfulness, yes, faithfulness and . . . and, even more boringly and simply, love."

I sensed that she was in exactly the same relaxed state as during the previous evening. It would have been very easy now to put my arms round her, draw her to me, kiss her. She would have let it happen, I was sure. Very easy and utterly impossible. We could hear the hiss of the fire in the great stone stove, the rustle of a branch against the window. Within her eyes, focused on the dancing flame, shadows were deepening.

A log exploded, a shower of sparks fanned out onto the floor. She turned her face toward me, spoke in a voice that was suddenly grave.

"The other day I found a letter from Otar. I expect you brought it. . . . The first real letter in thirty years. He talks about those very things: exclusive attachment, faithfulness, waiting. He says he's ready to wait. To change his life completely. Come back to this territory where he was once ordered to reside. Live in Mirnoe. With me. And leave if the other one ('the man who must return,' he calls him) did come back . . . "

Her lips were half open; she was breathing in little gasps, as if she had been running. That was precisely the impression she gave me, of a race, a headlong flight that would end in a collapse, a long cry of pain, tears.

In clumsy haste I asked: "And are you going to reply?"

She gave me an astonishingly lucid, almost hard, look: "I already have."

"And . . ."

"And the answer's no. For the one who must return will return. Otherwise love's nothing but a glass of water gulped down, the way our fair Alexandra used to describe it."

She smiled, got up, went in search of her coat. Emerging from my torpid state, I held out the long cavalry greatcoat for her. Its folds gave off a cold, wintry breath. With casual warmth she bade me good night, kissed me lightly on the cheek. Only the tiny quivers at the corners of her mouth betrayed what she was managing to control.

I stayed outside until she had reached the front steps of her *izba*. She walked slowly, giving the impression of holding in check an impulse to run, to escape. The beam of the flashlight she swung distractedly back and forth across the path sometimes veered upward, and its light collided with the bleak infinity of the sky.

I ARRIVED BEFORE the start of their concert to witness the rehearsal unobserved. The old marriage ritual was already more or less known to me. What I particularly wanted to see was the tentative emergence of the roles, the haziness of forgotten movements suddenly being reborn in the bodies' memories. I was curious to hear the ancient voices, blending together little by little, overcoming the silence of some years. . . . I walked around the *izba,* formerly the village library, where the performance was due to take place, and crouched down beneath a window. One of the four panes was broken and had been replaced with plywood, so I could clearly hear what was being said inside.

All Mirnoe's "regulars" were there, seven women

who had put on long dresses from another era, flowered shawls. White, russet with gilt threads, black. Country finery whose worn fabric and faded colors could be made out even through the window. Katerina, tiny and shriveled, wearing a kind of orange *sarafan* that was too big for her, was conducting the choir with her back to the window. The others, arranged in a semicircle, their arms folded over their chests, were obediently following her instructions. The status of conductor fell to her quite naturally: Katerina was the only one with complete recall of the songs and steps that made up this ritual from days gone by.

They were preparing to perform it at the request of the great Leningrad scholar that I was in their eyes, an unintended fraud.

As it happened, the rehearsal was frequently interrupted by brief but vehement arguments on the subject of myself. Or rather my relationship with Vera. There were two opposing opinions: though I was viewed by some, the majority, as a dangerous and unprincipled intruder, in the eyes of my two supporters I became "a good fellow who chops wood better than most." Katerina, destined by her role to be the mediator, cited my exemplary conduct when I carried her through the forest, but nevertheless agreed that "folks from Leningrad these days have hearts of stone, like that city of theirs."

If the truth be told, passing judgment on my worth

as a human being was for them no more than a way of alluding to the contradiction that none of them dared face up to: if they learned that a new love affair had just put Vera's faithfulness toward her soldier at risk, their world, founded on the cult of the victims of the war, would have collapsed. And yet, as women who had suffered so much loneliness, they could only wish for her to be loved, even if it meant succumbing to an untimely, tardy love, with scant regard for tradition, a love that would be both her salvation and her ruin. I noted that the two evenings spent in Vera's company had sufficed to establish me in the minds of the women of Mirnoe as an ardent and persistent lover. At no point did they refer to the age difference between us. Since almost all of them were in their eighties, they perceived us as a couple in which my three months' beard perfectly complemented the youthful glow that Vera's features radiated.

"With love it's like the spring floods," declared Katerina. "There's no help for it. Even if it's fall now. . . ."

Several voices objected, but she banished their protests with an elegant rippling movement of her hands, and the choir struck up, already in almost perfect unison. And when, as the soloist, she made her responses to them, in an astonishingly clear and firm voice, their earlier squabbles seemed trifling, just a little warm-up for the vocal chords.

"He'll come from beyond the sea, beyond the White

Sea, vast and chill," sang Katerina. And the choir took up the theme: "From beyond the White Sea he'll come."

"He'll come bringing the dawn. He'll find it where the sun goes down. He'll bring it for you, from beyond the sea." Her voice became increasingly dreamy, and the choir responded in an even more remote echo, marking the distance the traveler had come.

"Zoya, you're always a little bit behind. Do try to keep up. Otherwise they'll think you've gone to sleep." Katerina stopped the choir. The women stirred. "They'll think . . ." *They* was me. I slipped along under the window to approach the building from the front, and before knocking at the door, I made the sound of heavy, noisy footfalls on the front steps. The conductor of the choir came to let me in. Her pale cheeks were colored by the excitement of the dress rehearsal.

At first, I found the first public performance less moving than that rehearsal. The presence of an audience, in the shape of myself, made the old women more stiff, needlessly solemn. But on the other hand, perhaps by finally losing themselves fully in their performance, they had attained the hieratic ponderousness that this ceremony of bygone days demanded—a heaviness of plowed earth, the rigidity of wooden idols, the pagan totems their ancestors used to nail on the porches of their *izbas.* Acting out the scenes of the marriage, they moved with the menacing weight of living statues.

Their voices, in contrast, rang out with a disarming sincerity and sweetness, with an expressiveness that, as always with amateur performers, revealed more of their own personal emotions than those of the characters.

At one moment this distance between the performance of the ritual and the truth of the voices became painful. The bodies were acting out the fiancé and his chosen one boarding a ship and preparing to cross the White Sea. It was easy to imagine that, in reality, this epic voyage was taking place not at sea but on the lake that bordered Mirnoe, and that the place "where the dawn arises" was the little hill on the island. The old actresses slowly rocked their arms to imitate the movement of the oars. It occurred to me that Vera might at this very moment be on the water, returning to the village in her boat. They were acting out this crossing, too. With touching devotion. But their voices did not deceive.

"He'll come despite mists and snows to love you," they sang. But their lips bore witness to what they had truly lived through themselves: men who went away and disappeared forever in the thick smoke of war, men returning covered in wounds, to die beside the lake.

"And your house will be filled with joy, as a hive is filled with honey. . . ." Yet the tone of those voices spoke of *izbas* buried under the snow, where they themselves had come close to ending their days.

"He'll come," caroled Katerina in a stronger voice that marked the approaching end of the ceremony. "He'll come, his arms weary from the voyage but his heart on fire for you. . . ."

Suddenly we saw Vera.

She had clearly arrived well before this last part of the performance and had remained unnoticed, leaning against the door frame, not wanting to interrupt the choir.

It was her flight that gave her away. The door creaked, we looked around, and there she was, her hand on the handle. Her face was tormented into a frozen smile, her eyes growing wider with suppressed tears.

The choir fell silent. Only Katerina, whose eyesight was very weak, continued singing: "He'll come despite storms and snows. He'll come and take you to where the dawn arises. . . . He'll come . . ."

I ran out, but Vera was already far away. She was making her escape, no longer trying to hide, heading blindly toward the willow groves beside the lake. I tried briefly to catch up with her, then went back to wait for her near her *izba*. To my great surprise, she was already at home, busily packing a suitcase.

"I'm going to Archangel for three days tomorrow.

It's the city festival, you know. They've invited all the local celebrities. Including me, of course. Mind you, I'm not sure in what capacity. Probably as a heroic teacher with a strong reek of the soil about her. No matter. It'll be a good chance to buy medicines for the old women. If you're still here and you notice any of them are unwell, I'll leave you the doctor's address just in case. He's a good dozen miles from Mirnoe, but if you cut around by the lake you can reach him in an hour. . . ."

Then I recalled these festivities: they were due to begin that month and carry on, from one cultural event to the next, through into the following year, with the publication of an illustrated volume for which my contribution on indigenous traditions was awaited. "On the marriage ceremony," I thought, "as sung by old women who lost their husbands or sons over thirty years ago. . . ."

The following morning I saw Vera setting off. She was wearing a pale pink coat, with her hair put up in a chignon. The acrid tang of her perfume, Red Moscow, hung on the clear, frozen air for a moment. Her gait, her whole demeanor, betrayed the fierce determination of a woman ready to try her luck one last time.

"What rubbish!" I immediately interjected into that train of thought. "Just a woman walking briskly, for fear of missing one of the trucks that pass the crossroads by the empty mailbox . . ."

After her departure, I experienced almost relief, a kind of deliverance. I began serenely preparing for my own departure at last, namely by tossing a few books and notebooks into the depths of a suitcase and then roaming far from the village within the somber, luminous cathedral of the forest.

IN ONE OF THE DESERTED VILLAGES, this half sheet of lined paper, fastened to the door of what had been the grocery store: "Back in an hour." Faded ink, message almost illegible. A door closed on a house abandoned long years ago. And this promise to come back within the hour.

"All that remains after the death of an empire," I would often tell myself when, during those hours of walking, I came upon the traces of the era we had treated so poorly. The era that had sought to transform this northern land into a great collectivist paradise and had now left behind an immense solitude, enlivened by a few unintentionally ironic notices, soon to be indecipherable.

The deep indigo of the fir forests, the russet of the undergrowth, the intense blue when a dazzling burst of sunshine occurred amid the gray of the sky. And from time to time the dark, heavy glint of water in a pond down in the hollow of a thicket. The black, the ocher, the blue. These were what one really discovered after the end of an era. . . . After our time spent on this earth, I thought as I returned home that evening. My suitcase was almost packed now, the house cleared of the few traces of my stay there. Life in Mirnoe would continue peacefully after my departure. It was amazing, infuriating, obvious.

At such moments the days I had spent there seemed to me incomplete, ruined by my clumsiness: quite unresolved, this encounter with Vera, with her past, with what had briefly arisen between us. What else? The words to describe it flowed in, pretentious, cumbersome: affection, desire, jealousy . . . I continued on my way, my gaze lost in the somber gold of the fallen leaves, the white of a cloud captured by the lake. These restlessly recurring sights expressed much better what it was that had brought us so indefinably close.

Each morning, I determined to follow through with that trip to the White Sea. And each time I shied away from it. On the first day, for the good, vaguely hypocritical reason of not wanting to leave the old women unattended. They really had no need of me. Like model children, they were making every effort not to fall ill while Vera was away

("So as not to die!" I joked cynically). Faithful to her instructions, I replenished their water supplies, chopped wood, went to see them in turn. Even the frailest of them seemed boundlessly full of the joys of spring. I promised myself I would go to the White Sea the next morning.

I was thwarted by a memory at once benign and threatening.

Halfway along the road to my objective, I came to a village I did not at once recognize. Deserted *izbas,* rye-straw roofs in shreds, a pond overgrown with reeds. Gradually it all came back to me, Gostyevo, Katerina's village . . . The feeling of entering a forbidden place arose within me, and grew steadily as I approached her house. The little bench on which I had sat while waiting for the outcome of the discussion between her and Vera. The front steps where the boards had groaned under my feet.

The disagreeable feeling came over me that I was violating a place, desecrating a past. The door yielded readily. By the light of that sunless day the interior of the room seemed blurred, fraught with suspicion. That same miniature edifice stood at the center of the room: the little house-within-a-house. A pair of old felt boots with broken heels stood beside the stove, like sliced-off legs, ready for walking. Overcoming a murky, superstitious fear, I opened the little house's door. A very small bed, a tiny stool, a narrow table at the bedside. And, lying on the ground, a yellowed envelope. "An old letter she used to reread every evening," I thought, mindful of the clichés of books and films.

No, it was a kind of final message drawn up by this woman who expected to die alone. In large, painstaking handwriting she gave her surname, her first name, her place and date of birth. On the front, she had noted, in a column, the first date of each month, doubtless so that it would be possible to establish the approximate time of her death. . . . And at the bottom of the page, in the same rather schoolgirlish handwriting, was added this request: "Please, if possible, plant a wild rose on my grave. My husband, Ivan Nekiforovich Glebov, who died for the Fatherland in August 1942, loved these plants."

On leaving the miniature *izba,* I took the path back to Mirnoe, the one we had followed when we brought Katerina to her new house.

I arrived at nightfall and decided to leave Katerina's letter at Vera's house, adding a little note to it. Would it be right to return this sad text to the old woman, now that her situation was so different? In fact I was using this rescued envelope as a pretext for going into Vera's house for the space of a minute. Doors were never locked in Mirnoe.

In the main room, nothing had moved since our last meeting. "A nun's quarters, or an old maid's," was the malicious thought I had, sensing that the judgment was accurate as regards the sparseness of the place but essentially wrong. For a dense and troubling feminine presence could be felt here, despite the apparent order. Through the half-open bedroom door, I saw a high bedstead, village style, with iron posts. A blouse hung from a hanger close to the stove. . . . No, in the end, it was not my spying on these intimate details that offered the key to Vera's secret. It was rather the memory of a woman hauling in her nets on the lakeshore by the light of an August sunset. Her body uncovered by the bunching of a wet dress. Another woman, her nakedness gleaming blue in the moonlight outside the bathhouse door one night in September. Another, the one who passed me an oar, whose wood retained the warmth of her hand. Yet another, sitting at the far end of the bench, her eyes fixed on the crossroads. And the one I had tried to hypnotize with my hesitant caresses.

All these women were there. Not in this room, but in me; they had become a part of my life without my being aware of it. Only yesterday Mirnoe had still seemed to me no more than a brief episode, soon ended.

Before leaving, I turned to make a mental note of the silent intimacy of this room. Strangely enough, this final glance reminded me of Katerina's miniature dwelling. I pictured Vera alone here in the depths of winter, trying to see out through the windows coated with ice.

Not giving myself the time to think, I took hold of

the edge of the long bench and pushed it farther into the room. Then I moved the big table to match. Furniture of thick planks, colossally heavy. Now when one sat at the very end of the bench, one no longer saw the distant crossroads but the expanse of the lake, already filled with a purple sky.

On the third day, I did not go, misled by the constantly changing light. The west was overcast with low, leaden clouds, promising an onslaught of snow. Then a breeze arose from the south, bringing sunshine; the trunks of the fir trees turned red and warm, oozing resin. Out of the wind, it felt like spring, like the start of an endless day on the brink of a new life. With the carelessness of travelers who give no thought to the return journey, I hurried off along the track that led to the White Sea. An hour later, the sky darkened, the air became permeated with the acid tang of ice, and I retraced my steps. To await the next illusory spring.

Just as I was attempting to ford a watercourse, once again a luminous mirage lit up the forest. I was familiar with this narrow river, which had the transparency of strong tea. We used to cross it when heading for Mirnoe and taking a short cut through the forest. But its level had risen markedly, and the ford I had had occasion to cross in the past was currently hidden beneath a long rippling stretch of water weed. I kneeled down, drank an icy mouthful, as scalding as alcohol, then, with the bad conscience of a giant destroying the fragile beauty of the waters and the delicately ribbed sand, I began to move forward, anxious not to stir up the bottom, where a few dead leaves lay. Now the sun had broken through, it was spring again and all this a carefree ramble, with flashes of dazzling bronze shimmering in the depths of the stream.

I was within a few paces of the far bank when the sound of running reached me. The spot where I set my foot down was the river's deepest point; the water now slid very close to the top of my rubber boots. I froze in an irresolute and farcical posture, unable to advance, not daring to retreat. Then the crashing of broken branches rang out and petrified me even more. I imagined that some wild animal, hunted, hunting, or hunting me, was about to emerge onto the riverbank.

I took a halting step backward and turned toward the footfalls as they drew ever closer. In a quick spasm of fear, all those hunters' tales flashed through my mind: a wounded elk, in the agony of death, crushes those who stand in its path; a bear disturbed at the start of its hibernation becomes a man-eater; a pack of wolves in pursuit of a stag . . . Should I run away, filling my boots with water, or take advantage of my terrified paralysis, which, with a bit of luck, might make me invisible? Although my glance was a frenzied one, I had time to notice an ants' nest on the bank the noise was coming from.

The branches of the young fir trees stirred; a living form emerged, ran headlong toward the water. It was a woman. A moment later I recognized Vera. She knelt down twenty yards upstream from where I was stuck, drank jerkily, stood up, gasping for breath like an animal at bay. Her face, on fire from running, looked incredibly youthful, simultaneously reinvigorated and blinded by an unknown agitation—on the verge of a great shout of wild joy, or of bursting into tears, I could not tell which. I was about to call out to her but felt too ridiculous, grounded as I was in fifteen inches of water, and decided first of all to extricate myself, then to catch up with her on the path. I did not have much time, for as soon as she had caught her breath, she hared off once more, crossed the river at the ford I had failed to find. I saw she was wearing ankle boots with high heels, hardly designed for the forest. The water spurted up beneath her feet, then settled, carried an eddy of sand in my direction. She was already running through the forest; within a few seconds the wind hissing in the tops of the fir trees obliterated the sound of her flight.

Suddenly a trickle of icy water filtered into my left boot, sharp as a razor. I came to my senses, dragged my bogged-down feet along, headed toward the bank with no more thought of the ford. And when, calmed down by walking, I tried to understand Vera's appearance, a notion came into my mind, which showed me the degree of idiocy of which a man is capable when he thinks he is in love. Quite seriously the notion occurred to me that she had left the city for fear of not seeing me again before my departure, that she set great store by having one more meeting with me. . . .

The sight of Mirnoe, of its *izbas* clustered beneath a sky once more clouded over with gray, made me less sure of my own importance. "Probably one of the old women has fallen ill. Vera heard about it on the return journey and, devoted as she is, hurried home, cutting through the forest. In any event, it wasn't for the sake of my pretty face. . . ."

An hour after my return, someone knocked at my door. On the front steps I saw Vera. With the light pink coat thrown over her shoulders, she wore a knee-length skirt and the elegant blouse I had seen draped over a hanger beside the stove in her house. Her hair was braided into a broad plait, interwoven with a scarlet ribbon. Her eyes, slightly enlarged by a pencil line, fixed me with a smile that struck me as both aggressive and vulnerable.

"The official celebrations are over," she said, in rather too theatrical tones. "But maybe we could celebrate the city's anniversary ourselves now. Come and see me. The dinner's ready."

She turned on her heel and walked away, apparently unconcerned whether I was following her or not. Far from certain as to the reality of what was happening and, above all, of what might happen, I hurriedly changed, snatched up the great cape of tent canvas, and rushed outside. There was a risk that the figure in the overcoat might vanish at any moment in the already dark street.

We were afraid of one another. Or rather, afraid *for* one another. Afraid of seeing the other one make a false move that would have shown up the whole duplicity of this candlelit dinner. Afraid that the other might suddenly draw back, observe the room, the table with dishes and bottles on it, the body just embraced. Afraid of reading in the other's now alienated look: "What on earth are we up to here, in this remote house at the end of the world, in this night battered by a wild wind? What are we laughing for? This laughter of ours is such a sham! What is this hand doing fondling the back of my neck? What games are we playing?"

A single pointed glance, a single gesture out of place, would have been enough to transform this tête-à-tête into an insane charade. Its end was known: we were going to spend the night together. It was the whole point of the scenario, but it was looking increasingly improbable. Increasingly expected and impossible. This woman smiling at me, laying her head on one side to squeeze my hand between her cheek and her shoulder. Impossible. Like the sugary taste of the lipstick she had just left on my mouth.

We were afraid one of us might stand up and murmur, with a yawn: "Fine. That was all just a joke, wasn't it?"

From time to time, this fear showed through briefly in a tone of voice, a gesture, and we hastened to skirt around it. We had a choice between two clichés: sometimes this dinner took on the air of a well-lubricated peasant-style meal, with noisy mirth and the natural familiarity of close neighbors, sometimes the atmosphere was reminiscent of a student celebration. We felt in league with one another. We had to transform this old *izba,* the wind rattling the windowpanes, the tenuous warmth of this room, the warmth of our two bodies, into an amorous encounter, to blend this precarious mixture into a fleshly alloy. Our hands, our bodies, went through the motions; our words quickly overcame each onset of silent embarrassment. Only our eyes occasionally exchanged a chilling admission: Why are we doing this? What's the point of it all?

This play-acting remained resistant to reality until the moment when we found ourselves standing, face to face, on the threshold of the bedroom. There was a silence, swiftly broken by the wind's wild moanings, the crackle of the logs in the fire and, more deafening than these sounds, our disarray. Despite the dullness of intoxication, one very clear notion struck me: This woman doesn't know what to do next, she no longer knows her part. The memory of a very youthful affair surfaced within me, the shade of a first lover, and of this same ignorance in the face of desire.

She overcame her hesitation almost immediately. Became a mature woman again, a woman who knows, passed off her hesitation as the voluptuous slowness of a body influenced by drink. She even gave a little snort of laughter when I tried to help her undress. Naked, she drew me to her, swept me into that high double bed I had so often imagined. There was even the scent of male eau de cologne I had imagined. My own. And the fragrance of her hair, her skin, dried birch leaves steeped in the steam of the bathhouse.

At the first embrace, this self-possessed woman vanished. In the act of love she did not know who she was. Statuesque feminine body with a young girl's inexperience. Then a muscular, combative passion, imposing its own rhythm on pleasure. And again, blankness almost, the resignation of one asleep, her head thrown back, her eyes closed, biting her lip hard. A remoteness so complete, as if of a dead woman, that at one moment, drawing away from her, I grasped her shoulders and shook her, deceived by her stillness. She half opened her tear-stained eyes, smiled at me, and, respecting our game, her smile was transmuted into a drunken woman's hazy grin. Her body stirred. She gave herself with the frenzy of one who seeks either to win a man's forgiveness or to mock him. Several times, the ecstasy twisted my features into grimaces of male gratification. At these moments, I met her look, one of astonishing compassion, such as only mothers and the simpleminded can bestow.

Right up to the end, I managed to forget who this woman was. And when I remembered, the pleasure became unbearable in its sacrilegious novelty, its terrible carnal banality.

The end came with the slamming of a door or a window, at first we did not know which. Vera got up quickly, crossed the bedroom, went into the hall. When, half dressed, I caught up with her, she was sitting on the far end of the bench, her bare body covered by her long cavalry greatcoat. She was staring out of the window and seemed totally disconnected from what had just passed between us. "But nothing at all happened," the thought even came to me, in a momentary hallucination. This woman had spent her whole life glued to this bench, waiting for a man to return. . . . I mumbled an ambiguous greeting somewhere between an attempt to stay and a farewell. She murmured, "Good night," without stirring, without taking her eyes off the window.

OUTSIDE, HIGH IN THE SKY, the wind is feverishly chopping the yellow of the moon and the greenish flocks of clouds into pieces. The air has a sobering effect, and with sardonic clarity, I find myself comparing this flickering landscape to a romantic film with a lush moonlit setting, sped up by a mad projectionist to the pace of an animated cartoon. When I get home I cram the stove with large logs; the fire burns easily, merrily. And happiness, earlier clouded by the improbability of what I have just lived through, finally wells up without restraint. I have just made love with such a woman! And already there is a casual and obscene echo: "I've slept with a woman who spent thirty years waiting for another man!" With an effort I manage to feel ashamed of this.

I am twenty-six, an extenuating circumstance. An age when one still takes pride in the number of women one has possessed. With the return of postcoital cynicism, it is more or less this notion of keeping a tally that occurs to me. But I do manage to avoid the crassness of counting this woman alongside the others. Such a woman! Again I reflect on the absence of any man in her life. With self-satisfaction, I note my status as the lucky one.

I fall asleep in a state of perfect mental and physical contentment, the epitome of what a woman can give to a man prepared to ask nothing more of her.

My satisfaction is so serene that on waking and recalling Otar's words, I cheerfully accept his definition of man-as-swine. This facile joy lasts barely an hour. The memory of a day returns: a boat caught between the sky and the heaving water of the lake, a woman pulling firmly, rhythmically on the oars, the body of a dead person in my arms. . . . Projected onto a different scale of things, I suddenly feel very small, petty, clinging to a pleasure that is already beginning to fade. Compared with that long crossing of the lake, I am nothing more than a minor mishap. This notion upsets and alarms me: I should not have ventured into a dimension that is so far beyond me. I am saved by the physical memory. The supple, dense warmth of a breast, the welcoming spread of a smooth groin . . . Throughout the morning, I contrive not to stray beyond the refuge of these bodily sensations.

A gray wall of rain comes down. Unfaltering, not a moment's respite. I picture Vera on the way to her school. "A woman who gave herself to me." A hot surge of male pride, in the lungs, in the stomach. An urge to smoke a cigarette, gazing out into the street, an urge to be blasé and melancholy, despite the joyful turmoil stirred up by the thought of this conquest. At about three in the afternoon, after hundreds of different imaginary scenes, this other: her return home along flooded roads, she in her *izba,* in her kitchen, preparing to cook this evening's meal, a dinner for the two of us. . . . The pleasant routine of a relationship beginning.

At about four, the notion of her solitude after my departure. The rain stops, the sky is polished steel, pitiless. She will walk along this street, soon to be covered in snow. Her footprints, the only ones in the morning, the only ones on the way back from school. She will remember me. She will often think of me. All the time, perhaps.

This realization is vaguely daunting, but flattered vanity prevails for the moment: myself as the distant lover, gone without leaving a forwarding address.

At six o'clock, there is a knock on my door. It is Zoya, the tall one. She enters with slow ceremony, only stepping into the room after the third invitation, in accordance with custom. Sits down, accepts the offer of tea. And when the tea is drunk, takes a newspaper out of her pocket, not the local weekly but a daily paper from Archangel, which she unfolds and spreads out carefully on the table. Accounts of the celebrations for the city's anniversary, photos of well-known personalities born in the area who have distinguished themselves in Moscow, Leningrad, and even, in the case of this bald-headed engineer, at the Baikonur Cosmodrome.

I leaf through the pages, I express my admiration for the engineer: born in a tiny village on the White Sea, he is now the designer of a space communications system! The insistence of Zoya's stare makes me uneasy. She glares at me with condescending hostility, as much as to say: All right, stop your idle chatter and let's cut to the chase. I fall silent, she turns the page, points at one of the photos.

An elderly man, photographed with his two granddaughters, as the caption explains. A round, fleshy face, a fatherly expression. His jacket is weighed down by the broad disks of several decorations. "A typical Soviet apparatchik," I say to myself, and the caption tells me that this is a certain Boris Koptev, party committee secretary in a big Moscow factory. . . .

"It's him."

Zoya's voice betrays a sudden breathless weakness.

She recovers at once and repeats in the firm tones of a verdict: "Yes, that's him, all right. . . . The man Vera's been waiting for all her life. . . ."

Her story is concise, and I feel as if I am listening to it with my whole body. It reverberates like a blow, like a fall, like a shock wave, leaving no space within me, nothing untouched.

The final battles of the war before Berlin's outer defenses: that day dozens of men fall from a pontoon gutted by an explosion. Soldiers from the corps of engineers engaged in preparing for crossing the Spree River. Among these bodies torn to shreds, drowned, is that of Boris Koptev. News of his death is conveyed to the next of kin in a terse notice, a standard form of which millions of copies were printed: "Reported missing in action. . . . Died a hero's death." His only remaining next of kin is his mother, soon to be carried off in the famine of 1946. And also this strange fiancée, who will retain, like a holy relic, that earlier death notice (sent in error, as the military authorities later inform her) in which the soldier was described as "reported missing in action." And so the waiting can begin.

But what also begins is a new life for Koptev, freshly discharged from the hospital: repatriation, celebrations in Moscow, the heady sensation of being the victorious hero, acclaimed at every step, the host of female faces beaming at him, all those women ready to give themselves to men still whole and free, as he is, to these male survivors, now so rare. . . . Once an obscure young kolkhoznik, he has become a glorious defender of the Fatherland; once a clodhopper directed to remain in his hamlet in the far North like a serf, now he is taken to the capital, where his medals open the doors of the university to him, guarantee him a career, erase his rustic past. It is only this past he dreads. On the road back from Berlin to Moscow he saw villages in Byelorussia in a state of devastation, peopled by starving ghosts, walking wounded, and children with rickets. Anything but that! He wants to stay among the victors.

Zoya has already been gone a moment. Her story is still unfolding in my mind, a sequence of facts easy to imagine, familiar from so many other eyewitness accounts, embodied by so many men and women I have encountered since childhood. A soldier's return. The era I was born in was entirely devoted to this dream, the joy of it, its ruination.

Did he ever chance to think of Mirnoe, of the love he had left behind amid the soft and weary snows of April? Very rarely, in all likelihood. Such was the shock of discovering Europe, for one who had never before seen a city and multistoried houses. And then Moscow, a powerful drug of novelties, a fabulous stimulant of temptations. It was not that he forgot, no, he quite simply no longer had time to remember.

As she was leaving, Zoya paused on the threshold, looked me straight in the eye, and declared: "So that's how it's been, our history," adding, in almost severe tones: "Our history, for us here. . . ." Her tone excluded me, calmly but definitively, from this history. Only the previous day, such a rejection would have pained me, I was feeling well and truly rooted in Mirnoe. Now I am relieved by it. Incautious rambler that I am, I have strayed into the rear of an ancient war.

After Zoya has left, I embark several more times on reconstructing Koptev's life, picturing the thirty years that have turned him into this tranquil grandfather and worthy Party functionary. Then comes the moment when I realize I am thinking about him so as not to think about Vera. And I realize I have neither the courage nor the powers of reasoning now needed to imagine the feelings of this woman who has spent her whole life waiting for a man. Emptiness, pained amazement, timid fury, nothing more.

It is very cold. I go outside in search of logs piled up beside a shed. The sky is an icy purple; the mud beneath one's feet resonates, a harbinger of frost. The wood rings out too, like the notes on a keyboard. I prepare to go inside, but suddenly at the end of the street I see the beam of a flashlight slowly zigzagging over the ruts in the road. Vera . . . I step back, squeeze into the shadow against the timbers of the *izba.*

It seems I need this humiliating fear to make me understand what this woman is now. A voice, the same sordid little voice that was congratulating itself over my having "slept with" such a woman, cries out within me: "Now she's going to cling to you!" Taking the moral high ground, we consign this voice to the outer periphery of our consciousness, amid the slime of our instincts. Doubtful, this. For often it is the first to make itself heard, and is very like us.

The flashlight beam sways gently, drawing inexorably closer to my hiding place. Obviously she is coming to see me, she wants to talk to me, unburden herself, share her grief, weep, be comforted by the man who . . . All at once, I realize that for this woman I am now the person I have become since last night. I am possibly the only man she has known since the departure of the soldier. She no longer has anyone in her life. Her footprints in winter, in this street. In her *izba* the window from which you can see the crossroads, the mailbox. She no longer has anything or anybody to wait for. So, me!

The spray of light spills over the front steps to my house, passes within a yard of my feet. She is going to knock on the door, sit down, settle in for an interminable conversation interrupted by sobs, embraces I shall not have the courage to resist, the extortion of promises. It will all be hideously false and perfectly real, brimming with harsh, pure truths about her ruined life. She needs help a thousand times more than the old women she looks after.

The advancing beam does not slow down, passes my house, moves away. She must be going to prepare wood and water for a bath, so one of the old women can take it tomorrow. This domestic observation gives me a breathing space but only at the surface of my fear. Deep down, the obscene little voice is on the alert: "She'll call and see you on the way back. She'll settle down, probably keep quiet, play the part of the woman who has complete faith in your honor. You're cornered. She'll come and see you in Leningrad. She'll cling to you like a leech. The love of older women. Especially a woman like that. In her eyes, you'll take the place of the other one. You already are the other one she thought she was waiting for. . . ."

I go in, light the fire but prefer to stay in the dark. All the little stove door lets through is a glowing strip of pink. If someone (someone!) comes, I shall pretend to have gone to bed already.

In reality, it all happened differently. The minute-by-minute reconstruction, the timed storyline of that night of cowardice was put together much later, in those moments of painful honesty when we meet our own gaze, one more pitiless than either the scorn of others or the judgement of heaven. This gaze aims straight and shoots to kill, for it sees the hand (mine) cautiously lowering the latch on the door, the fingers cradling the metal to avoid any kind of click, the door locked—in this village where bolts are never shot. The electric flashlight beam once more sweeps through the darkness, traveling up the street. I withdraw, cock my ear. Nothing. The one whose fate I dread sharing disappears into the darkness.

In reality, that is all there was: fear, the icy logs against my chest, the endless wait a few steps away from the shaft of light as it sliced up the muddy pathway, then the vigil in the *izba,* the anxiously muffled actions, the latch lowered slowly, as if in the hypnotic slowness of a nightmare. No, objectively, there was nothing else. The fear of seeing a woman come to me, her face ravaged by sobbing, of being contaminated by her tears, by her fate, by the inhuman and henceforth irremediably absurd seriousness of her life. A life as pointless as the hammer blows that had just now rung out in the distance. What was it that was so urgent and necessary to construct in total darkness?

One more detail that crops up close to midnight when the likelihood of her coming begins to diminish. ("Although in the state she's in, even at midnight . . .") I cover the shade of my table lamp with a towel. I switch it on and notice the book she lent me a month before. A book on linguistics by Saussure that I have not even opened. A book-as-pretext: that was still the time when I was seeking by every means possible to win the friendship, affection indeed, of this woman. I was enamored of her, in love, I desired her. All these words now seem incongruous, impossible to utter. The fear recedes. I manage to reflect, to ponder the bizarre features of our lives. This borrowed Saussure proves that, even in situations as strange as ours, the stages in a relationship are always the same: at the beginning a talismanic object, a message in a bottle, the feverish hope of what it may lead to; at the end, this useless volume one no longer knows how to get rid of. . . .

Again I study the Archangel newspaper Zoya left on the table. The photo of Koptev, the art of being both a grandfather and a good Party man. It suddenly strikes me that, if there is any logic to existence, his flat, round physiognomy ought to be associated with Vera's face. For they could have (should have?) formed a couple. . . . Impossible to fit them together. "She's much younger," I tell myself, feeling confused. "No, she's not, there's scarcely three years between them." I get in a muddle, trying to grasp what it is that makes these two beings absolutely incompatible. The only way to picture them together is to turn Vera into a formidable Muscovite matron, with heavy features, a satisfied look, the holder of a university chair, a Party member. . . . Just the contrary of what she is. "She's not part of that world," I conclude lamely in the end, feeling that I am much closer to the world of the Koptevs myself. This affinity reassures me, liberates me, distances me from Mirnoe.

At about two in the morning, a great sense of relief. I know I must get up very early, steal out of the village, make my way rapidly to the crossroads, hop onto a truck and, once at the station in the district capital, take the first train to Leningrad, to civilization, to oblivion. Which is what I shall do. I feel resolute, energetic. I switch on the lights in the room, no longer hiding, and within five minutes I have closed my suitcase, which for weeks now I have not managed to pack. No further question of racking my brains: this part of the world has made me ill, its past, the woman who has preserved its spirit. Now my cure is at hand. At the first whiff of the sharp air on the Nevsky Prospekt . . . For a minute I wonder if it would not be more elegant to leave a note. Less inelegant, let us say. Then I decide to just slip away.

During the few hours of sleep left to me, I wake up often. It is very cold. The darkness outside the windows has the sheen of ink, that of the great frosts. In one of my waking moments, I think I have gone deaf. Not a breath of wind, the fire in the stove dead, the silence of the interstellar spaces, icy, absolute. I lack the courage to go out and bring in some wood. In the hall, I snatch up the old military cape. I lay the canvas over the top of my blanket. The fabric is all worn, scorched here and there by fire, but, oddly enough, the thin layer of it warms me better than a fleece-lined quilt would have. A dream comes to me. The story one of the old women of Mirnoe told me: her husband, killed in the snows of Karelia in cold of forty below, the obsessive urge she has since then to heat up a bath for him. In my dream, a soldier lies naked in the middle of a white plain. He opens his eyes, I wake up; on my frozen cheeks I feel burning tears.

7

THE FIRST GLANCE OUTSIDE, well before sunrise, is a plunge into an unknown world. All is pale and blue with hoarfrost; its suede has petrified the trees, the walls are encrusted with its crystals. The road, bristling with muddy ridges only yesterday, is today a long, smooth white track. The dry stems of nettles beside the old front steps rear up like silver candelabras. I open the door long enough to take a deep breath, trying to hold onto the icy intoxication of this beauty to the point of giddiness. This air, I sense, could drug me all over again, make me forget my departure. . . . I must leave as quickly as possible.

Suitcase in hand, I reach the lakeshore while the sun, still invisible, can be sensed behind the forest. The earth, blue-tinged, is still of the night. But the whitened crowns of the tallest firs are overlaid with a fine, transparent gilding.

I quicken my pace to break the spell of this imminent luminescence that holds me back. The first trucks will soon be driving past the crossroads. But the magic of the moment is everywhere. Every step produces a distinctive resonance of shattered ice. One could stop, melt into this time where there are no hours. I look back: a faint hint of smoke hovers above the chimney of the house I have just left. Poignant gratitude, fear of not being able to tear oneself away from this beauty.

Now my course will move away from Mirnoe, cast off the enchantment of its last stages: the little bathhouse *izba,* the undergrowth amid the willow groves . . .

Suddenly, in the perfect stillness of white and blue, a dark movement. But there is nothing abrupt about its appearance. A long greatcoat, a woman's face. I recognize her, there she is, her presence at that spot is entirely unremarkable, I could have encountered her there yesterday, and the day before. Leaning forward, she is trying to push out the boat trapped in the ice, in the frozen clay of the shore. She seems totally preoccupied by the attempt.

I keep walking, through sheer muscular inertia, sunk in a hypnotic numbness, already picturing the scene that is bound to take place: she will hear my footsteps, straighten up, come toward me, with a look increasingly impossible to bear . . .

She hears my footsteps, stands up, greets me with a brief inclination of her head. Her eyes have an expression I know well. They do not really identify me; it will take them time to admit me to what she sees. She repeats her greeting, a simple replica of the first, returns to her task.

I am free to leave. But I step off the road, walk down toward the shore.

The boat is hardly moving. The ice around its hull has been crushed by the woman's boots. The clay is very red; footmarks print themselves on the white like traces of blood. I look for somewhere to set down my suitcase in this mixture of ice and mud, then I put it on the seat in the boat. And take hold of the gunwale. The woman presses down on the opposite side, I respond to her action, the vessel starts to rock, embarks on a jerky, barely perceptible forward motion.

Next, this supple sliding, the sound of the thin layer of ice being broken by the hull as it is propelled into the water. The woman is already on board, she stands upright in the stern, a long oar in her hands. I climb in too, not knowing whether it is to retrieve my suitcase or to . . .

I am seated in the bow, with my back to the goal of our crossing. As though I did not know, as though I did not need to know where we are heading. Facing me, she does not look at me, or when occasionally our eyes meet, she seems to be observing me across immensely long years. The ice breaks under the oar, the clattering of the drops has a metallic sharpness.

"A fine trap," I say to myself, realizing that it was inevitable. A sly, do-as-you-would-be-done-by logic decreed that a reckoning between us should take place. This will happen: tears, reproaches, my clumsy attempts to console her, to wriggle out of it. But first the woman will do what she has to do on the island, then we will return to Mirnoe and I'll fulfill my duty as her unique friend, the only man she has known in thirty years.

The notion is as far-fetched and as obvious as this whole white world that surrounds us. A bridal white, immaculate, terrifying in its purity. Even the lengths of pine that form the cross are swathed in crystals.

She is going to the island because of this cross laid over the thwarts of the boat. I remember her words: "Next time I'll take the cross. . . . " So next time is today. A cross for Anna's grave. Anna, whose body traveled there in my arms. And last night's hammering was the wooden arms being nailed on. And the flashlight beam marked the cross being carried down to the boat. Why take it at dusk? Why not this morning? I suddenly grasp what kind of woman it was who yesterday turned carpenter. A woman who could only hold on to life by fashioning this symbol of death. She will thrust it into the earth and then begin talking to me, weeping, trying to keep me in her life, where there are more crosses than living people. The main post strikes me as disproportionately long, then I realize that this is the base that will be buried in the earth.

The island is white. The church, all frosted over, seems translucent, ethereal. The earth surrounding the cross, now bedded in, is the only dark patch in this universe of white.

We walk down to the shore, resume our places in the boat without a word. At one moment, I think of speaking, defusing the serious reckoning that lies ahead with a few neutral words. But the silence, too all-embracing like the nave of a vast cathedral, restrains my voice, diverts it inward toward the feverish thought tormenting my mind: how to tell this woman that in order to share her fate even for a short while, one would have to learn how to live in this afterlife that is not the life the rest of us live, one would have to rethink everything: time, death, the fleeting immortality of a love affair. One would have to . . . The sky above the lake is unbearably vivid, the purity of the air swells the lungs so much that one can scarcely breathe anymore. I long to get away from this white wilderness, to find myself once more within the smoky confines of our Wigwam studio, amid the hubbub of drunken voices, the press of bodies, of frivolously trivial ideas, of swift couplings with no promises made.

We circumnavigate the island. Soon the red clay of the shore, the willow groves . . . She will step ashore, look long into my eyes, begin to talk. What shall I be able to say to her: death, time, fate? She is a single woman who, quite simply and humanly, no longer wants to be so. But this white infinity she carries within her will never fit into the snug shell of a Wigwam.

The cold makes me feel the stillness of my body. I sit huddled on my seat with my suitcase between my legs. The idea comes to me suddenly of escaping as we land. Leap ashore, pull up the boat, seize my bag, shout out a good-bye, go. The movements she makes with the oar are spaced further and further apart, as if, guessing my intent, she wanted to delay our arrival. I know that in any case I would not be capable of flight. A most inconvenient lack of cynicism!

At this moment the bow of the boat gently encounters an obstacle. I turn, open my eyes wide. No willows, no trampled red mud. We are landing at the old jetty on the far side of the lake. Before I can grasp what has just happened, Vera steps out onto the boards that sag gently on top of the old piles. I follow her automatically, my suitcase in my hand, onto the narrow landing stage.

She looks me in the eye, smiles at me, then kisses me on the cheek and returns to the boat. And she is already moving her oar as she says: "Like this you're quite close to the town. You can catch the eleven o'clock train. . . . May God keep you."

Her face seems older to me; a lock of silver hair slips down over her brow. And yet she is utterly brimming with a fresh, vibrant youthfulness that is in the process of being born, in the movement of her lips, the fluttering of her eyelashes, in the lightness of her body as the boat begins to bear her away. . . .

I wave my arm in a pointless farewell; her back is turned, and the distance is growing rapidly. I step forward to the end of the jetty and with sorrowful intensity say to myself that my voice could still carry, and I absolutely must tell her . . . The silence is such that I can hear the soft lapping of the waves set off by the boat's departure, coming to rest amid the wooden piles.

I have never before made my way to the town starting from this spot. The footpath from the landing stage climbs upward, and when I glance behind me, I can see the entire lake. The island with the pale smudge of the church and several trees above the churchyard, the blue-gray undulations of the forest, the roofs of Mirnoe, which have lost their dazzling whiteness. Soon the hoarfrost will begin to melt, and they will look like the roofs of one village among many, waiting for winter.

In the distance, the boat on the icy surface already appears unmoving, and yet it is traveling forward. The trace of clear water spreading behind it grows longer, extending toward the infinity of the snow-white plains, toward the dull glow of the sun. And farther off, amid the icy fogs of the horizon, suddenly a space lights up, beyond the fields and the treetops of the forests. The White Sea . . .

Above the dark line of the boat I can still make out the figure in a long cavalry greatcoat. Despite the distance, it seems to me as if I can hear the tinkling of the ice as it breaks. The same ringing sound that fills the glowing expanse of the sky. Now the sound ceases, as it does when the oar suspends its thrusting motion, comes to rest. I believe I can make out the gesture of an arm waving above the boat, yes, I can see it, I hasten to respond . . .

And the sound resumes, faint, unwavering.